The Brother Quest

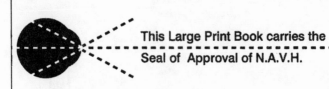

This Large Print Book carries the
Seal of Approval of N.A.V.H.

The Brother Quest

Lori Handeland

Thorndike Press • Waterville, Maine

SEP 15 2006

Published in 2006 by arrangement with Harlequin Books S.A.

Thorndike Press® Large Print Romance.

The tree indicium is a trademark of Thorndike Press.

The text of this Large Print edition is unabridged.
Other aspects of the book may vary from the original edition.

Set in 16 pt. Plantin by Myrna S. Raven.

Printed in the United States on permanent paper.

Library of Congress Cataloging-in-Publication Data

Handeland, Lori.
    The brother quest / by Lori Handeland.
        p. cm. — (The Luchetti brothers ; #2) (Thorndike
Press large print romance)
        ISBN 0-7862-8825-6 (lg. print : hc : alk. paper)
        1. Large type books. I. Title. II. Series: Thorndike
Press large print romance series.
PS3558.A4625245B76 2006
    813′.54—dc22   2006014928

For Randy Pierce
Fifth-Grade Teacher
Oriole Lane School
Thank you for teaching my sons
so many things.
They are both the better
for having known you,
as is every child who has
spent a moment in your classroom.

Dear Reader,

I hope everyone is enjoying THE LUCHETTI BROTHERS series. The amount of mail I received after writing *The Farmer's Wife* convinced me that readers loved those Luchetti boys as much as I did.

Being an only child, I've long been fascinated with sibling relationships. I ask a lot of questions of friends and family. I observe my husband's relationship with his two brothers and now my sons' relationship with each other. I have to be honest. I don't understand it. Why can't everyone just get along?

When I ask this, my husband, my sons, my friends laugh right in my face. So I've begun exploring the love/hate relationship between siblings with the Luchetti brothers.

Colin and Bobby Luchetti shared a room growing up. So it's natural that when he's in trouble, Bobby sends Colin a note. The note sends Colin to Wind Lake, Minnesota, to a preschool called Chasing Rainbows and a woman named Marlie Anderson.

Marlie and Bobby were pen pals, until Bobby disappeared. A captain in the U.S. Special Forces, Bobby was last seen in Afghanistan. Unfortunately, Marlie knows nothing about it. Colin decides to hang around Wind Lake on the off chance that Bobby will show up. In doing so he gets a lesson in small towns, little kids, loyalty and the power of love.

With cameo appearances by some of your favorite Luchettis — as well as a few new ones — a guinea pig named Houdini and a few familiar dalmatians, I hope you enjoy this second install-ment of THE LUCHETTI BROTHERS, *The Brother Quest*.

Lori Handeland

For information on future releases and a chance to win free books, visit my Web site at www.lorihandeland.com.

CHAPTER ONE

If anything ever happens to me, go to 445 Briar Lane, Wind Lake, Minnesota.

Colin Luchetti read the cryptic note for perhaps the hundredth time. He would know the precise, anal retentive handwriting of his brother anywhere.

Something *had* happened to Bobby, but no one was sure what. He was a captain in the U.S. Special Forces and the leader of a twelve-man A-team. Nevertheless, he had disappeared in Afghanistan about two months ago. Neither his superiors nor his men had any clue where he'd gone.

The note would have been cause for celebration, indicating that Bobby was still alive, except the thing had been postmarked before Colin's brother disappeared.

But the date on the envelope raised another question. Had Bobby known he was in danger? If so, why hadn't he written a better letter?

Colin had called Bobby's boss and informed him of the note, but the man had been unimpressed.

"It's not like Osama or one of his goons could sneak into camp and make off with your brother, Mr. Luchetti."

"No? From where I'm standing, Osama seems to sneak around at will."

"Since you aren't standing here, how would you know? When we have news of your brother, we'll be in touch."

The call had been terminated. Colin wasn't surprised. He rubbed authority figures the wrong way — always had.

As a foreign correspondent for the *Chicago Dispatch*, Colin was living his dream. During a long, boring childhood in the heartland of Illinois, he'd imagined seeing the world and writing about it.

The prospect of staying in Gainesville and being just one more Luchetti brother had been unappealing. He'd decided he wanted to be famous. After eight years of busting his hump in places very few people wanted to go, he was well on his way to getting what he wanted.

But he'd had to turn down a plum assignment to Pakistan and take vacation time — something he had plenty of, since he rarely used it — to go searching for his brother. Why Bobby would send him to Godforsaken, Minnesota, Colin had no idea. But since it was the only clue available, here he was.

He glanced through the windshield of his rented car toward the redbrick house with 445 in large black numerals on the front. The sign just below the numbers read Chasing Rainbows Preschool. What was going on here?

Colin would have understood if his brother was shacked up with some Nordic bimbo. He'd have kicked his ass, but he'd have understood.

Except Bobby was not the type to go MIA in one place, then turn up somewhere else with a woman. He hadn't gotten to be a Special Forces officer by being irresponsible. For Bobby, the army was his life, his career there as important as Colin's was to him. Which only made his sudden disappearance all the more disturbing. Bobby Luchetti had not earned the family nickname GI Joe because he liked to play with dolls.

Shaking his head, Colin got out of the car and approached the preschool. The windows were decorated with handmade American flags and bright red-and-green apples.

He understood the apples — this was a school, after all — and since it was near the end of August, the flags made a certain kind of sense. Labor Day was only two weeks away. What else did they have to look forward to around here?

On the front door a sign said Welcome, Friends, so he turned the knob and stepped inside.

The floor was covered with little bodies. For an instant his neck prickled, until he saw that they were sleeping.

Weariness washed over Colin. He wanted to grab a mat and lie down, too. He'd gotten on a plane in Paris . . . yesterday? This morning? Tomorrow? His mind was too jet-lagged to do the math.

Colin glanced around. Several walls had been removed to construct a single open area at the front of the house. A long hallway led toward the backyard. There was a single doorway on the opposite side of the room.

He caught the sound of a voice and followed it, picking his way through the maze of children until he reached a door that was ajar. Colin pushed it open and froze.

A woman knelt on all fours, head and shoulders stuffed beneath a table, fanny up in the air.

"Come out of there right now, you hear me? This is *not* funny."

Her blue jeans were worn thin at the

seat, emphasizing a round, ample backside. A bit too ample to be considered trim, but Colin was getting mighty sick of the no-ass model types he'd dated. Just once he'd like to take a woman out to eat and actually see her eat.

When had that started to bother him? *Why* did it bother him? He'd squired some of the most beautiful women in the world to places most people only read about. If they had no asses, who was he to complain?

Suddenly the woman dived forward. He heard a thump, like a head hitting metal. "Ouch! You're going to pay for that."

Colin frowned. Was that any way to talk to a child?

He cleared his throat.

She jumped and banged her head again, then backed out from underneath the table. Glancing up, she rubbed what must be a good-size knot by now.

She was very young, maybe eighteen or nineteen. Her blond hair fell in a soft straight wash past her shoulders. Her skin was pale and clear, full cheeks flushed with pain, embarrassment or heat, he wasn't sure which.

She wasn't exactly pretty. In fact, she appeared to still have her baby fat, as his mom would say. Large-rimmed glasses — severely out of style and not at all flattering — framed light-blue eyes surrounded by thick lashes.

His fingers itched to remove those glasses and get a better glimpse of those amazing eyes, but she scrambled to her feet and lunged for the phone.

"Hey, relax," he ordered.

She hesitated, glancing toward the room full of sleeping children, then back again. Her smooth skin creased into a frown that spread from her ample mouth all the way up to her forehead.

"Who are you and what are you doing in my preschool?"

Colin lifted his hands in the universal gesture of surrender. "I'm looking for . . . a . . ."

His voice trailed off. He wasn't sure what to say. Bobby wasn't here. He'd be a little hard to miss. Maybe Colin was in the wrong place.

The girl tilted her head, and her hair slid across her T-shirt, drawing his attention to the purple dinosaur on her chest. It was an amazing chest.

He forced his eyes back to hers. Lucky for him she was too young, too innocent or maybe too preoccupied to notice his faux pas. Why on earth was he ogling the spectacular breasts of a woman who was not only too young but not anywhere near his type? Sure, he was sick of no-ass models, but he'd never had a taste for large-boned Viking women, either.

Though her frown had disappeared, she still stared at him with her eyebrows lifted, though it was kind of hard to tell since they were so blond they were almost invisible. Women of his acquaintance would have felt the need to dye those eyebrows or pencil them in. That she hadn't done so interested Colin more than it should have.

"You'd better state your business or I'll be calling Chief Moose."

The image of an actual moose wearing a policeman's hat walked through his mind, but he shook it away.

"If you're so worried about intruders, maybe you should lock the front door."

"No one locks their doors in Wind Lake."

If Colin hadn't lived the first eighteen years of his life in another land of the unlocked door, he might have been surprised.

"Where *is* the lake?"

"What lake?"

"*Wind* Lake."

"There isn't one."

15

"Isn't Minnesota the land of ten thousand lakes?"

Her lips twitched. "You've been reading license plates."

He hadn't had much choice. The drive out of Minneapolis had been full of them.

"The Indians named the place," she said. "In the spring and summer, we're tornado alley. In the winter, blizzard bay."

His confusion must have shown because she elaborated. "Hence the name Wind Lake — as in lake of wind. Or at least that's what the Sioux called it in their language, which was too difficult for us white folks to pronounce, so we changed it."

"I see," he said, though he didn't.

Her gaze darted to the floor. She let out a soft but intense, "Gotcha, you little son of a gun," and fell to the floor behind the table. A scuffle ensued.

"Um, should you really be treating him, or her, like that?"

"What?"

She climbed slowly to her feet and blew her hair from her face with an upward puff of air from her lips. Her right hand was hidden from his view by the tabletop.

"I know I'm not a teacher or anything," Colin continued, "but you seem to be treating that kid a little rough."

"Kid?" She giggled and lifted her hand. Draped over her palm was a . . .

"Ugh." Colin shuddered. "That's the biggest rat I've ever seen."

Her giggle erupted into laughter, the force of her mirth making her chest jiggle better than anything he'd ever seen in the opening credits of *Baywatch*. But the sound was so inviting, Colin found himself distracted from the view. When she laughed, he wanted to laugh with her, an uncommon occurrence for him.

Colin rarely laughed. In his world there wasn't much he found funny. Starvation, war, overpopulation — nothing to chuckle about there.

He'd been a solemn child, and he'd become a sober man. Still, he might have laughed along with this woman — if he hadn't been so grossed out by the rat-thing in her hand.

"This is Houdini." She stepped over to the counter and popped the animal into a cage. Twisting the lock, she shook her head. "The disappearing guinea pig. Blink and he'll be out of there and under the furniture before you can say, 'Eek!' "

She contemplated him for a moment. "Where are you from that you don't know a guinea pig from a rat?"

17

Now that he got a good look at the critter, safely confined, Colin could see it wasn't a rat. It only looked like one.

"We didn't have many pets where I grew up."

His mom had always said there were enough animals in the house — referring to himself and his four brothers. The farm dogs had stayed outside, and they'd never been very petlike. The thought of Eleanor Luchetti allowing a guinea pig anywhere near her was ludicrous.

The places he'd been living since he'd left the farm had rats the size of dogs, which might in some way explain his unreasonable aversion to large rodents. If there'd been any guinea pigs, they'd have been lunch — for the rats and the people.

"Too bad," she murmured. "Kids should have pets."

Colin shrugged.

"You really thought I was chasing a child around under there?" From her expression, she obviously couldn't decide if she should be amused or insulted.

"Sorry."

She waved her hand, dismissing his apology. "You were concerned. I wish more people would speak up if they feel uneasy about the things they see. We might have less abuse, fewer kidnappings."

She smiled, and Colin was left dazzled and wondering how he could ever have thought she wasn't pretty. She had perfect teeth, white and straight. Her parents had obviously been able to afford braces. Unlike his own.

"Now, who is it you were looking for?"

"My brother."

"Brother?" Her smile faded. "I'm sorry, but I can't let you take any of my kids without permission from their parents, even if you are his brother."

Colin's tired brain didn't catch her meaning for several seconds. "Oh! No. My brothers are all older than you are, Miss . . . ?"

"Anderson. Marlie Anderson."

The name fit her. Soft, sweet and Swedish. Or was it Norwegian?

Colin shook his head. What difference did it make? Damn, he was tired.

"Then I don't understand why you think you'll find your brother *here*. What's his name?"

"Bobby Luchetti."

From the way Miss Anderson's beautiful blue eyes widened behind her great, big glasses, he *had* come to the right place.

★ ★ ★

A chill went through Marlie. She'd been uncomfortable from the moment she'd seen this man's face, and she hadn't been able to figure out why. It seemed as if she knew him. But she'd never seen him before.

She sat on the edge of the table and his brow creased with concern. He took one step forward, hand outstretched as if he was going to touch her. She probably looked as if she might faint.

Not that crawling out from under a table to discover that a stranger had strolled through a room of sleeping children who were in her care shouldn't upset her. Since intruders in Wind Lake were as scarce as a green Christmas, something like this had never happened before. However, his presence in her school no longer upset her; his identity did.

"Which one are you?" she managed through a tight throat.

"Colin."

Marlie ran through her knowledge of Bobby's many brothers. Colin, the foreign correspondent.

He resembled Bobby around the eyes; they had the same shade of brown hair, though Bobby's was a lot shorter. And

20

while Bobby had the muscular build of a lifetime soldier, his brother's body was long and lean, as if he liked to run marathons, though Lord knew why.

His perfectly coiffed hair, handsome face, piano-man fingers and smooth way of talking made her think he spent most of his time sipping martinis in rooms lit by chandeliers. She'd half expected him to introduce himself as "Luchetti, Colin Luchetti."

"How do you know Bobby?" he demanded.

She ignored the question. She had a few of her own that were much more important. "Why would he be in Wind Lake?"

"I was hoping you could tell me. You haven't seen him? Heard from him? When was the last time he was here?"

"I've never met Bobby Luchetti in my life."

Colin rubbed his forehead. "Miss, I don't mean to be rude, but I just flew here from Paris —"

"Well, la-di-da," she muttered, then clapped her hand over her mouth.

Marlie usually kept her sarcastic comments to herself. A lifetime living in Wind Lake had taught her that a smart-mouthed girl got into trouble, and a smart-mouthed preschool teacher ended up with very few students. As a result, all of Marlie's perfect comebacks took place in her own head.

But this time she'd actually spoken out loud. What was the matter with her?

She was confused and a little bit afraid. There was no reason for Bobby's brother to search for him here. Heck, if he was searching for him at all, that couldn't be good.

Colin didn't even acknowledge her rudeness. Instead, his gaze flicked over her shoulder. His eyes widened. "Um, your . . . uh, that thing . . ."

She spun around just in time to see Houdini escape from his cage and race away.

"Darn!" She threw up her hands. "I give up. Let him hide all night. Let him never come back." She lowered her arms to her sides in defeat. "But the kids will cry."

"Miss Anderson, I'll help you look for your rat-thing —"

"Guinea pig," she corrected.

"Whatever."

His mouth twisted with distaste. He really seemed to dislike her "rat-thing." Strange behavior for a man who'd been raised on a farm.

"I'll help you," he repeated, "but first,

can you tell me how you know my brother?"

"We're pen pals."

That stumped Mr. Not-a-Hair-Out-of-Place. "I don't understand."

"We've exchanged letters. Frequently. Or at least we did until last spring."

Marlie stifled a sigh. Bobby had a busy life, an important job. She was surprised he'd written to her for as long as he had.

But what had hurt was that he'd stopped writing after she'd sent him her picture. She knew she wasn't pretty. In fact, she was downright plain, even dumpy.

But Bobby hadn't seemed interested in her in that way. He'd been lonely. He'd liked hearing about the children. When he'd asked for her picture, she'd sent him one. What difference did it make if she didn't resemble Britney Spears?

"What's happened?" she demanded.

Marlie never demanded. She didn't shout. She rarely swore. When folks in Wind Lake thought of Marlie Anderson, they thought of a sweet, sturdy, soon-to-be-old-maid schoolteacher. She was a comforting, sure presence in the lives of so many children, which was exactly what she wanted to be.

If she'd dreamed a few foolish dreams in

the privacy of her bedroom, so what? She was entitled. It wasn't as if Bobby would ever know she'd fantasized about him. She'd never planned on meeting the man and certainly never thought she'd meet his brother.

The urge to scream, shout, shake Colin Luchetti until he told her what was going on nearly overwhelmed her. Marlie clenched her fists and took one step forward. "Tell me."

Colin's eyes widened. "Relax, Xena. I will."

Xena? Warrior Princess?

Why did Marlie find the comparison pleasing? He was probably referring to the fact that she was as tall and strapping as Lucy Lawless, though she'd never be half as pretty.

"Bobby's missing."

"In action?"

"Not exactly. He went to bed one night and in the morning he was gone."

"And then?"

"Then they waited and they searched and they never found him."

"Is the United States Army in the habit of misplacing their captains?"

"You'd be surprised at what they misplace."

Marlie's eyebrows shot up. She lived in a conservative hamlet that didn't question the federal government — much. The idea that the army might not be as invincible as everyone liked to believe was not something Marlie wanted to dwell on. Especially these days.

"Why did you come here?" she pressed.

Colin opened his mouth to answer just as a small voice said, "Miss Marlie? Ned had an accident again."

Colin whirled, staring at the little boy in the doorway as if he were the renegade guinea pig.

Marlie didn't need to ask what Jake meant. The damp patch on the front of his sweatpants told the tale.

"Accidents happen, Big Jake," she said brightly.

"How come they always happen to me and Ned?" Jake hung his head.

Marlie wanted to scoop the child up and cuddle him close, but she needed to get him changed first. "Let's find your spare clothes, kiddo. That's what they're here for."

"Ned, too?"

"Ned, too," she agreed, even though Ned had no extra clothes, because there wasn't any Ned.

"Ahem."

She glanced at Colin. He was staring at his feet with an expression she could only describe as horrified.

"Houdini!" Jake shouted, and lunged.

The furry body shot off Colin's shoe and disappeared behind the filing cabinet. Marlie took Jake's hand.

"You're not going to just leave him back there, are you?"

She couldn't be sure, but she thought Colin inched closer to the door.

"What do you want me to do?" she asked. "I can't chase Houdini *and* locate Jake's spare clothes. Unless you'd like to volunteer."

"Sure."

Expecting Colin to pursue the guinea pig, Marlie was left openmouthed when he took Jake's hand and let the boy lead him out of the room.

CHAPTER TWO

Jake led Colin through the maze of still-sleeping children and down the long hallway to a set of wooden cubbyholes outside the bathroom.

Colin was still pondering the information that Marlie was Bobby's pen pal. Though Bobby had decent handwriting, he very rarely used it. Excluding the cryptic note delivered to his office, Colin could count on one hand the other letters he'd received from his brother.

Not that Bobby was lazy. Far from it. But there were so many other ways to communicate in this day and age, writing letters was nearly a forgotten art. The question remained — how had Bobby "met" Marlie?

Jake tapped his thumb to his lips as if he was thinking of sucking it but knew better. Colin wasn't sure how old the boy was. Younger than five to be in preschool and older than diapers — Colin caught a whiff of ammonia on the air — but not by much.

"Hey, kid, where's your pal, Ned?"

Colin glanced around expecting to find

another soggy, perhaps tearful, child trailing behind them, but the hallway was empty.

"He's right here." Jake lifted his hand and crooked his wrist, as if resting his arm along the back of invisible shoulders.

Invisible. Great.

Jake lifted his arm and pointed to a bag labeled JAKE high atop the other cubbies. "Help?" he asked plaintively.

Colin retrieved the sack and handed it to the boy. "Thanks." The kid removed a pair of sweatpants identical to the ones he wore, except these were red instead of blue, then disappeared into the bathroom.

He returned almost immediately. "Help?" he repeated.

"Sorry, I don't see any clothes for Ned."

Jake rolled his eyes. "Ned don't wear no clothes."

Colin, still jet-lagged and a little bit slow, stared at Jake until the light dawned. A *naked* invisible friend. Even better. In Colin's imagination his friends were always naked, too. Of course, those were girl-friends.

He put that thought right out of his head. Now was not the time and here was definitely not the place.

"You need help changing?" he guessed.

Colin swung his gaze to the office door, obviously hoping to see Marlie. Her shadow flitted back and forth beneath the overhead light. She must be chasing Houdini from one end of the room to the other and back again.

"I been dressin' myself since I was two, mister."

Colin heaved a sigh of relief. "Then, what do you need help with?"

Jake lifted his shoe. The laces were tangled into one huge knot. "My dad tied 'em triple 'cause I'm untied-shoe boy."

"Well —" Colin lowered himself to his knees "— I should be able to fix that."

He began to pick at the laces. It wasn't easy with short fingernails, but he managed — in about ten minutes. By the time Colin was done, there was a line for the bathroom. Boys and girls, large and small, blond, brunette and even one redhead, stared at him with sleepy, curious eyes.

"Who you?" asked a very small, extremely pretty, raven-haired young lady.

She appeared dressed for a tea party in a frothy pink skirt and a silky white shirt. Her shoes, or he should say shoe, matched the skirt and had an open toe and a tiny heel; her socks were trimmed with lace. He half expected her to pull pink lipstick out of the handbag hung over one wrist.

Now that he took a moment to observe, all the little girls were dressed like miniature models, while the boys wore jeans or sweatpants. What was up with that?

"Who *you?*" the girl repeated.

"Oh, I'm Colin Luchetti."

Every mouth fell open. One young man stepped from the line and his grubby hand crept toward Colin's slacks. Colin stepped back so quickly he slammed into the wall.

"Cappin?" the kid whispered, and touched his knee.

"What? Oh, no. I'm not the captain. I'm his brother."

"Crap." The little boy yanked his hand away as if Colin had a disease, leaving behind the imprint of his five stubby fingers.

Colin wanted to echo the expletive. However, all hell broke loose before he could.

The kid tried to get back into the line exactly where he'd left it.

The girl behind him said, "No come backsies, Victor. You left the line."

"Did not, Ka-*tri*-na!"

"Did, too."

Before Colin knew what was happening, they were shoving each other; a second later they were rolling across the floor. Jake barreled out of the bathroom, and the next kid in line barreled right in. The rest of them gathered around and shouted encouragement — girls for Katrina, boys for Victor.

Katrina was rough, despite the silvery white dress that bespoke a fairy princess. She was also bigger than Victor and somewhat mean. To make matters worse, there didn't appear to be any rules.

Guerrilla preschool. Whaddaya know?

Within a minute Katrina was sitting on Victor. When he struggled, she gave him a wet willy.

Colin smirked. The girl had to have brothers.

"What is going on here?"

The kids scrambled into line, backs against the wall. Katrina and Victor did, too, though the two of them continued to elbow each other viciously whenever Marlie's gaze shifted to someone else. Right now it had shifted to Colin.

He swallowed. "Uh, there was a disagreement about the rules of the bathroom line."

"There always is. And what were *you* doing, Mr. Luchetti?"

He'd been gaping like an idiot, but he wasn't going to admit it. "Supervising?"

Marlie folded her arms over her chest. Colin had to concentrate hard not to let his eyes follow the path of those arms.

"I don't know how things are done in Illinois, but in Minnesota, we do not allow children to brawl."

In Illinois, more specifically, in the Luchetti household, brawling was the most fun they ever had.

"Yes, ma'am," he muttered.

The kids giggled and Marlie shot them a glare. "Victor, Katrina. To the end of the line."

The two did as they were told without argument. Colin stared at Marlie with dawning respect. She'd been so gentle with Jake, so soft-spoken and calm, he'd wondered if she would have any control over the children at all. Now he knew. The no-nonsense side of her was unexpected and . . . interesting.

She reminded him of his mother, who had run their house with an iron fist. But then, she'd had little choice. With five boys, each a year apart, and a single girl a year after the boys, she had been forced to take charge or be obliterated. Once, Colin had believed his mother was the bossiest, most annoying woman on the planet. Now he understood she was merely amazing.

Twelve years away from home did wonders.

"Miss Marlie, he's your captain's brother." Katrina's voice was filled with awe.

Her captain?

Colin glanced at Marlie in time to see her cheeks flood with color. Was there more to her relationship with Bobby than a mere exchange of letters? Funny, Colin didn't like that thought one bit.

"We need to talk," he blurted.

"I know."

Colin headed for the office, pausing at the door to allow Marlie to precede him, except she wasn't there. Instead, she still stood at the other end of the hall.

"I didn't mean *now,*" she said.

"I did."

She gave him a glare that made Colin feel smaller than the smallest child. "Mr. Luchetti, preschool kids are like cuddly new puppies. Sweet, cute, fun, but don't ever turn your back on them for more than a minute."

Colin glanced at the children. Now that she mentioned it, they did look as if they might bite.

"When?" he asked.

"I close at five. I'll meet you at my house."

"Which is where?"

Every child pointed toward the front of the preschool. Colin raised a brow. "Across the street?"

She nodded. "Mine's the only house in the neighborhood that's a Colonial and not a ranch. It's the oldest one in Wind Lake. An Anderson founded this town."

Pride was evident in her voice. He couldn't say he blamed her. He'd often wondered where or when the first Luchetti had landed on these shores, but no one seemed to know. In his family, no one had cared.

"All right," he agreed. "I'll see you at five."

As Colin walked away, something small and furry shot out of the office and ran over his shoes.

His yelp was very undignified.

Marlie was smiling as the door closed behind Colin Luchetti. If it wasn't for his unreasonable fear of Houdini, she didn't think she'd care for him at all. His expensive tan slacks, lightweight chocolate-brown sweater and shiny leather shoes were as out of place in Wind Lake as the man himself was.

When he stared at her, she felt like a

specimen beneath a microscope. As if he were trying to see inside her brain and discover what made her tick.

He was a writer. Perhaps he stared at everyone that way. If so, he was no doubt lonelier than she was. Though with that face and body, she doubted it.

Marlie had no right to feel sorry for herself. She had friends. Plenty of them and good ones. She'd been born here. She'd no doubt die here, and that was fine with her.

In Wind Lake there were two kinds of people. Those who couldn't wait to get out and did so as quickly as possible, and those who loved the place and were devoted to it, never leaving, never wanting to.

This made the town a tight-knit, friendly community. Everyone knew everyone else and helped one another. Wind Lake had known for decades that it took a village to raise a child.

Life was slower here, safer; nothing ever changed. Marlie still had the same best friend she'd had in kindergarten.

As if the thought had conjured him up from thin air, Garth Lundquist stepped into the preschool. Six foot four and built like an oak tree, Garth was gorgeous and mellow as a spring breeze, unless someone he loved was in danger.

On their first day of school, Garth had shoved the bully who was tormenting Marlie into the mud. They'd been pals ever since. Even his marriage to Annika Kristofferson had not dimmed the friendship. Garth had loved Nika with all of his heart, and when she'd died from a burst aneurysm at twenty-two, part of that heart had gone with her.

"Daddy!" Jake launched himself across the room and into Garth's arms.

A flicker of pain crossed his face as it did every time he saw his son. Jake was a little-boy version of Nika.

The pain turned to guilt at the sight of Jake's pants — a different pair than those he'd had on when Garth had dropped his son off that morning.

Jake had just turned five, and while he could have entered kindergarten in the fall, Garth had chosen — based on Marlie's advice and his own concern — to keep him back a year.

Jake was a bed wetter, and Garth experienced no small amount of anxiety because of it. Marlie tried to tell him that some kids found it harder to stay dry than others, boys especially, but he refused to believe that the loss of Jake's mother hadn't damaged him. Maybe he was right.

36

Garth set Jake on his feet and patted the boy on the butt. "Get your stuff and round up Ned while I talk to Miss Marlie, hmm?"

Interestingly enough, while Garth agonized over Jake's inability to stay completely dry at all times, he'd taken Ned in stride.

Jake ran off to fetch the plastic sack full of wet clothes. Garth watched him go.

"It's not your fault," Marlie murmured.

"No?" He turned his intense gaze on her.

Garth was one of the few residents with dark eyes. Blue was the dominant eye color in Wind Lake, because if your ancestors weren't Swedish or Norwegian, you were from out of town. No one knew where Garth's nearly black eyes had come from. Some said the mailman, although never in Garth's hearing.

"If it isn't my fault," he continued, "how come I feel like it is?"

"Because you're a good dad. Guilt is part of the territory."

He shrugged and changed the subject. "I hear you had company today. Your captain's brother?"

Marlie blinked. Gossip in Wind Lake traveled like lightning to a golf club, but this was fast even for here.

Garth laughed, the sound rich and deep.

Though his eyes seemed permanently sad, his laughter was still the most beautiful sound Marlie had ever known.

"You shouldn't be so surprised, Peanut," he said, using the nickname he'd given her back when they were five.

She'd been more peanutlike then, as in small. Now she resembled a peanut only in body shape. But it did no good to complain to Garth about the nickname. To him she always had been, always would be, a peanut.

Of course when standing next to Garth, an offensive lineman would appear small — one of the reasons Marlie liked standing real close.

"A stranger in town is the most excitement we get, ya know."

"And how did you hear about this stranger?"

"He came into the café."

Garth ran the Wind Lake Café, a fancy name for the diner that had been Nika's. Until Jake turned three, Garth had kept him close while he cooked eggs in the morning, hamburgers in the afternoon and pork chops for dinner.

Then he'd discovered all the other Wind Lake kids went to preschool if they could, and nothing would do but that Jake went, too. Even though he missed his son something terrible all day.

"Poor guy was on an airplane." Garth shook his head, sympathy in every line of his face. "The food on them is pitiful these days, but I fixed him right up."

"Does everyone know he's in town?"

"Pretty much. But *why* is he in town?"

"You didn't get that out of him?"

"Nope. And not for lack of trying, either. He was on his cell phone, then he pulled out a computer and clattered away awhile. Hated to bug him when he was working. What kind of work does he do, anyway?"

"He writes."

"Children's books?"

Marlie snorted. "Does he look like a children's book writer to you?"

"I don't know. What does one look like?"

"Never mind. He's a foreign correspondent."

"He writes letters to foreigners?" Garth teased. "I guess someone has to."

Marlie rubbed her forehead. It had been a long day. But then, they all were. "He writes for a newspaper — in Chicago, I think — about foreign things."

"Who cares about foreign things?" Garth asked with the typical tunnel vision of a life-long Northerner. "Why is he here?"

"Bobby's missing."

Garth's eyes widened. "How?"

"I'm not sure. Colin's coming over to-night."

"Colin, hmm?" Garth waggled his brows.

Marlie snorted. "Yeah, right."

As if anyone who looked like a super-spy would be interested in her.

Garth leaned over and kissed Marlie's brow. "Peanut, if he has any taste at all, he'll snap you up before his brother does."

She hugged him and he hugged her back. Garth could raise her spirits nearly as high as the children did. She wished she could do the same for him, but some spirits could not be lifted.

He gave her one final squeeze, then got right down on the floor to read the kids a book. They climbed all over him and set-tled in close. Every child at Chasing Rain-bows loved Garth. What wasn't to love?

When the story was done, he tucked Jake beneath his arm like a football and rushed back to the diner. Shortly thereafter, parents began to arrive and the usual chaos ensued.

Though Chasing Rainbows was billed as a preschool, it was also a day care. Before school and after, Marlie watched kids so their parents could work.

At five after five she still hadn't found Houdini, and there were two kids who hadn't been picked up — Jeffrey and Janice Hoffsteader.

"Grab your things," she told the twins. "You're going home with me."

It wasn't the first time, and it wouldn't be the last. Their mother would know where to find them.

Marlie didn't like to leave the guinea pig on the loose, but it wasn't as if he'd stay in the cage. Most mornings her first order of business was a Houdini hunt followed by pellet patrol.

Ah, the glamour of her life. She didn't know how she could stand it.

The thought disturbed her, and as she and the children crossed the street, Marlie had a short talk with herself.

Her life was exactly as she wanted it.

Well, almost.

She'd dreamed of having children — a lot of them — and she did. Only they weren't hers.

She'd dreamed of a home and a family. Marlie stopped on the sidewalk in front of the house. This was her home, her family, her mother. Things could be worse.

No one ever had to know she was a virgin.

CHAPTER THREE

Colin arrived at the Anderson residence early. He didn't have anywhere else to go.

He'd had lunch at a rustic but clean diner, which appeared to be the only restaurant in town. After deflecting the questions and ignoring the curious stares, he'd checked his messages — both voice and e-mail — then made a few calls about Bobby.

Still there was nothing.

He phoned home. No one answered, so he left a message asking his mom to call when she got in.

His parents were understandably upset. When they'd received word from the army informing them that Bobby had disappeared, they'd tried to reach Colin. Unfortunately he'd been on his way from Uzbekistan to Belfast.

By the time he'd gotten in touch with his mother, she'd been hysterical — not only because Bobby had disappeared, but because Colin had managed to miss his brother Aaron's wedding to the ex-stripper who'd had his baby thirteen years ago.

Although life in Illinois had always bored Colin to tears, it appeared things had become far more interesting lately.

Colin parked his rental car in front of Marlie's house. He would have sat there until she arrived, but a woman stepped on to the porch and motioned for him to come inside. When he shook his head, she waved what appeared to be a wooden spoon at him, then retreated, leaving the door wide open. Colin shrugged and followed.

The house wasn't as large as the one he'd grown up in, but he'd lived on a dairy farm amid a family of six children. Their three-story farmhouse had been huge, yet still not big enough.

The Anderson home consisted of two bedrooms on the ground floor, a kitchen, full bath and living area. He had no idea what the second floor held. Although he was curious, an occupational hazard, he wasn't rude enough to go upstairs and look around as he had downstairs.

He found the woman, whom he assumed to be Marlie's mom, bustling around the kitchen. From the number of pots and pans on the stove, she was expecting company. From the heavenly smell wafting through the house, he hoped it was him.

"You must be Colin." She glanced over her shoulder as she stirred a big, steaming kettle.

He smiled and nodded. Mrs. Anderson was so short she had to rise on tiptoe to check a pan on the back of the stove, so thin there was no way she ate much of what she cooked. Her hair was pure white, just like his mother's, though hers had been twisted into a bun, instead of wound into a braid. But while his mother's hair had lost color prematurely, Mrs. Anderson's face matched her hair.

Colin frowned. She appeared to be at least seventy, but how could that be if she was Marlie's mother? Perhaps she was Marlie's grandmother.

"I'm Julie." She set the spoon onto a plate and turned. "Marlie's mom."

Huh.

Before he could ponder the mystery further, she scooped up a pitcher and two glasses with expert fingers. "Time for *Jeopardy!* Follow me."

Moments later he was seated in the living room, martini in hand, as she kicked his butt and that of today's big winner on elderly America's favorite game show. She'd also managed, he wasn't sure how, to talk him into a friendly wager on the game.

He could kiss that money goodbye.

"Would you like a refill?" Mrs. Anderson eyed his half-empty glass.

What he'd like was for his brother to walk through the door and inform him that his disappearance had all been a big paperwork snafu. Then Colin could catch the next plane to anywhere but here. Since that didn't appear likely, Colin shook his head. "Not yet."

Her face fell. "You don't like them?"

"No. I mean yes. This is the best martini I've had in years, ma'am. It's just . . . I'm not sure how far I'll have to drive to find a hotel tonight. I didn't notice one in town."

"There aren't any. No one comes to Wind Lake that doesn't live here or have relatives. No need for a hotel."

That was what he'd been afraid of. Colin hoped he didn't have to drive all the way to the suburbs of Minneapolis to rent a place to sleep.

"Who is General Ulysses S. Grant?" Mrs. Anderson demanded.

Colin very nearly said, "The eighteenth president of the United States," before he realized *Jeopardy!* had returned from the commercial break.

"You can stay with us," she said.

"I couldn't."

"I insist. You look done in."

He felt done in. The jet lag was getting worse. The martini probably hadn't helped, but he *was* a lot more relaxed.

Taking his silence for agreement, she reached across the end table and expertly refilled his glass. "What is a paramecium?"

Colin gave her a quick glance, but she was talking to Alex Trebek, not to him.

Marlie stepped into the house, Jeffrey and Janice on her heels. The warm scent of supper wafted over her. She was starving. There'd been no time for lunch today. Not that she needed it.

Of course skipping meals wasn't the answer to losing the extra inches on her hips. But she had no time to exercise, no energy for it, either.

The low rumble of Colin Luchetti's voice answered the question of whose car was out front.

"Now for Double Jeopardy where the scores can really change."

And that answered the question of what they were doing. Her mother was hustling *Jeopardy!* again.

Marlie took one step toward the living room and the doorbell rang. Before she could even turn, Jeffrey and Janice were flinging themselves into their mother's arms.

"Sorry I'm late."

Candy Hoffsteader didn't appear sorry at all. She never did. Without so much as a thank-you-for-being-there, she handed Marlie the twenty-dollar fine — ten dollars per child — and took her children to the car.

Marlie was never sure what Candy did after work to keep her from picking up her children on time. The fine worked to keep most parents from showing up late on a regular basis. But for some, like Candy, it was just an excuse to do what she wanted, then pay Marlie later. She should be happy Candy had shown up before the twins were in bed this time.

She closed the door and leaned against it for a moment. If she had children, she'd never leave them wondering where she was, when she was coming, or *if* she was coming.

"You're late."

Colin's voice directly behind her made Marlie spin around with a yelp. He was so close her breasts slid across his chest. His eyes widened and he stumbled back. Her face went hot, as did other more embarrassing, less conspicuous places.

She crossed her arms, realized that only drew attention to the situation, so she forced herself to lower them, then looked him in the eye.

He had guts to stand there in his silk slacks and shiny shoes and tell her she was late. She'd been at work before 6:00 a.m. Nearly twelve hours later, she was just getting home. Marlie took perverse pleasure in the child-size handprint on his knee.

He glanced from her to the door, then back again. "Your mother said that sometimes you have to bring kids home. Is that what happened?"

She nodded. "Their mom just came."

"In most places Mom would be searching for another preschool."

"Wind Lake isn't most places. There is no other preschool."

"So you let her take advantage of you?"

Marlie gave a tired sigh. He *would* see it that way.

"No, I let her kids know that there's someone in this world who will never leave them behind. They can count on me."

"But they aren't your kids."

Why did everyone always feel the need to remind her that she was childless, husbandless, sexless?

Marlie shoved past him and walked into

the living room as her mother finished off her martini. The closing credits of *Jeopardy!* rolled, along with the annoying theme song.

"How much did you take him for?" Marlie asked.

Her mother grinned. "Enough."

Colin finished his drink. Seeing him with a martini in his hand made Marlie's brand-new James Bond fantasy return. Too bad she had no hope of ever being mistaken for a Bond girl.

He set his empty glass on the coffee table. "She cleaned me out."

"Give it back, Mom."

"No," Colin interjected. "I lost fair and square."

"He lost all right." Julie snickered in a very unsportsmanlike fashion. "Big-time."

"She's really very good." Colin didn't appear upset at losing big money. Of course, he probably had big money to lose.

"She ought to be," Marlie grumbled, and stepped into the hall to stash her purse in the closet.

"Why's that?"

Marlie shut the door and turned to find that Colin had followed her again. "Because she remembers every *Jeopardy!* since 1975."

"She must have an excellent memory."

"For certain things."

The drumroll announcing *Wheel of Fortune*, her mother's second-favorite game show, commenced. "Mom? When's dinner?"

"When your father gets home."

Marlie sighed and rubbed her eyes. When she lowered her hand, Colin leaned against the wall, frowning at her. "We can wait for your dad."

"You'll be waiting a long time."

"I don't understand."

"My mom may have a great memory for *Jeopardy!* but what she can't seem to recall is that my dad has been dead for ten years."

Colin straightened away from the wall and glanced toward the living room.

"Tom Cruise Missile!" Mrs. Anderson announced.

"A before and after," Marlie answered in response to his bewildered expression. "Tom Cruise. Cruise Missile."

"I knew that." He hadn't, but he didn't want to appear completely game-show challenged. "What I don't know is why your mom is waiting dinner for a dead man."

Marlie winced and Colin wanted to bite his tongue. He'd associated too long with people who had no time or inclination for niceties. But he hadn't realized he'd become one of them.

He began to apologize, something he seemed to do a lot around her, but Marlie shook her head, opened the door and beckoned him outside.

She led him to a wrought-iron bench beneath the huge oak tree in the yard, far enough away from the house that their voices wouldn't carry through the open windows to her mother. Though, from the volume of the television, the only voices Mrs. Anderson would be hearing were Pat and Vanna's.

Marlie sat and Colin did the same. His thigh brushed hers. She inched away. He fought the urge to follow.

She didn't want him to touch her; he wasn't sure why. That he still wanted to disturbed him enough that he stayed on his side of the bench.

"Does your mom have Alzheimer's?" he asked gently.

Her back stiffened. "Of course not! She's only fifty-five."

Colin opened his mouth, then shut it again. He wasn't sure what to say.

"I know, she doesn't look it and that's not a compliment. All the years of worrying about my father have taken their toll."

Why would Mrs. Anderson worry about someone who'd been dead for ten years? Of course she was still holding dinner for him, too. Colin gave up trying to figure out what was going on.

"You lost me," he admitted.

Marlie glanced out at the peaceful, suburban street. Colin remained quiet while she gathered her thoughts.

"My father was a truck driver. She hated him being gone so much, hated raising me alone and always being lonely. She'd sit in the living room most days and every night, staring out the window, worrying and waiting. That's how she got into the game shows."

Well, that made sense. Kind of.

"She made him swear he'd be home for my fifteenth birthday, but he was late. We waited and we waited. About midnight Chief Moose came to the door. I knew it was bad."

Marlie drew in a deep breath. Colin wanted to reach out, take her hand, make everything better, but there was no fixing the loss of her dad.

"He fell asleep at the wheel, driving too long, trying to get home on time. My mother had to be medicated straight through the funeral. Then she refused to believe he was dead. To this day, nothing will convince her otherwise."

Once again Colin didn't know what to say, what to do for her.

"She watches game shows all the time now. Keeps her mind on something other than the fact that he never does seem to come back."

"You were only fifteen?"

Marlie nodded. That would make her twenty-five now, not the eighteen he'd believed her to be. Why that news made Colin happy, he didn't care to examine.

"How did you manage?"

"The house was paid off by insurance. We had enough to get by, but no college for me." She shrugged. "I baby-sat to make ends meet. When I got out of high school, I started working at the preschool. The owner sent me to technical college, and when she put the place up for sale, I managed to buy it."

He was impressed. If there was a poster girl for making lemonade out of lemons, Marlie would be it.

"How does Bobby fit into all this?"

She smiled at the mention of his brother's name, and a twinge of some unidentifiable emotion — one he couldn't recall having before and did not want to examine now — shot through him. Colin clenched his hands and forced himself to listen. He had come here for information, and at last he was getting some.

"Last fall the children drew pictures to send in letters to servicemen overseas. Bobby wrote back to thank me. His letter was long, detailed, interesting. We began to correspond."

Which just didn't sound like Bobby.

Colin reached into the pocket of his pants and pulled out the note. Without comment he handed it to Marlie. She read the words and raised her gaze to his. "This doesn't make any sense."

Colin had to agree. If something happened to Bobby, what possible good could it do for Colin to come here?

"We're friends," Marlie continued. "Or as friendly as two people get by mail, but this . . ." She shrugged and handed back the note. "I don't understand."

Colin didn't, either. How could Marlie and Bobby be friends?

He didn't voice the question, because he knew as little about friendship as he knew about babies. He hadn't had many friends in his life. He'd been shy as a kid, curious and studious. He hadn't cared that he was a loner, because he'd had plenty of brothers to play with and so many books to read.

He'd done a lot of dreaming then — of the places he would go, the people he would meet, the stories he would write and the fame that would make everyone in Gainsville remember which Luchetti brother he was.

Colin had worked his way through Boston College, where he had been labeled a hick — the farm boy from Illinois. Alone and far from home, he'd bent over backward to appear dignified instead of raucous, knowledgeable rather than backward. But the scent of manure must have clung to his skin, because he'd never managed to fit in.

He'd never fit in anywhere, which was why he never stayed in one place long enough to feel out of place. He was good at his job; he was moving upward and onward, seeing the world and writing about it, which was all he'd ever wanted out of life.

Colin contemplated Marlie's profile. He didn't think she knew anything else about

Bobby, which only made him curious.

About Marlie, about Wind Lake, about what had been going through his brother's mind when he'd written that note.

Dinner was a livelier meal with Colin there than it had ever been with just Marlie and her mom.

Julie Anderson didn't even seem to mind that her husband hadn't shown up — for the thirty-five-hundredth-odd night in a row.

Most evenings Marlie ate too much in an attempt to make up for her missed lunch and her mom's lack of appetite. Conversation would be stilted to nonexistent as her mother stared at the front door, while Marlie did her best not to lose her temper and demand that Julie face the truth and snap out of it.

Such outbursts always led to her mother taking a sleeping pill and missing *Who Wants to Be a Millionaire?* The loss of her third-favorite show only made Julie harder to live with when she woke up.

But tonight Marlie's mom didn't glance at the door or the clock once. She was too enthralled with Colin's stories of his travels around the world. Marlie was pretty enthralled herself.

"You've been to Hong Kong?" Julie scooped another helping of boiled potatoes onto Colin's plate, then added *Kalops,* a Swedish beef stew.

"Several times." He stared at the steaming food as if he meant to protest, then shrugged and dug in.

While her mother quizzed Colin on the technicalities of the Chinese takeover from Great Britain — no doubt an entire category on *Jeopardy!* last week — Marlie cleared the table.

As she filled the sink with warm water and suds, she glanced out the window above it. The neighborhood children had begun to gather in the backyard.

"Mom, time for your show."

"Oh!" Julie jumped up. "Gotta go. First question tonight is for a million dollars." She scooted from the room.

Colin pushed back his chair. The steady clip of his shoes across the vinyl floor made Marlie's shoulders tense. He leaned over and set his plate next to the sink. Marlie could see his reflection and hers in the glass, the contrast between them stark. Dark to light, lithe to large, Bond versus the milkmaid.

He peered out the window, squinting, and the heat of him warmed her back. His breath brushed her neck; she shivered. Thank God he didn't notice.

"What are they doing?" He indicated the growing crowd of kids in her yard.

"Getting ready to play kick-the-can."

"What's that?"

She craned her neck so she could see into his face. "You never played kick-the-can?"

He shook his head and picked up a dish towel. "We played catch-the-escaped-pig, -chicken, -cow — whatever happened to get out of its pen that day."

"You should be really good at catching the escaped guinea pig, then."

He made a gagging sound, and she laughed, then handed him a plate. "I'll teach you how as soon as we're done."

"To catch a guinea pig? No, thanks."

"I meant to play kick-the-can."

"They'll let us play?"

She ducked her head, embarrassed. How did she explain to this suave world traveler that most of her friends were out there in the yard?

"They're, uh, well, they're waiting for me."

He was silent so long she finally had to look up. He contemplated her with the same expression she'd seen before — as if she were a fascinating new bug he'd discovered under a rock.

"Okay," he murmured. "But I think I'll watch."

Though she knew he meant the game, nevertheless goose bumps trilled over her skin at the husky, suggestive tone of his voice. She could think of quite a few things she'd like him to watch — and none of them were meant for children.

Marlie forced her attention back to the sink where it belonged. If she continued to daydream about Colin, she'd only wind up embarrassed, hurt or both.

Together they made short work of the dishes, and moments later stood on the porch watching the children chase each other through the trees. There were all ages, all shapes, all sizes, both sexes — but only one color. Wind Lake was pretty white.

Marlie hadn't even seen an African-American until she was six years old. Sometimes she worried that her kids weren't getting a true view of the world by living in Wind Lake. The town was isolated and a bit backward. But what was she supposed to do about it?

Breathing deeply of the night air, Marlie listened to the childish voices and pretended all these kids were hers. Having Colin at her side added fuel to the fantasy. What if he was hers, too?

Marlie shook her head. Pretty soon she'd be as delusional as her mother.

"Of course that's my final answer, Regis." Julie's voice carried through the front window and into the night. "You know something I don't?"

Colin chuckled. "How come your mom doesn't try out for one of those game shows? She's good."

"She'd have to leave Wind Lake."

"So?"

"She never has." Marlie shrugged. "I haven't, either, for that matter."

She felt him glance at her, sensed his astonishment. "Why not?"

The children spotted Marlie and let out a cry of welcome, running across the lawn through the fading rays of the sun.

She smiled and told him the truth. "Everything I need is here."

CHAPTER FOUR

Everything she needed was here?

Colin stared at the yard. He didn't get it. *What* was here? Some grass, a few flowers, a house that was older than all the others. A mother who would rather talk to Alex, Pat and Regis than her own daughter.

He shook his head. If he had to live in this town, he'd go insane. Wind Lake wasn't Gainsville and this small subdivision wasn't a dairy farm, but it made him claustrophobic just the same. He hoped he wouldn't have to hang around much longer.

"What should we play tonight?" Marlie asked.

Each child shouted the name of a different game, creating a mishmash of sound Colin couldn't decipher.

"All right. All right."

Marlie laughed, and Colin inched closer, drawn to the happiness in the sound. Many of the children did the same. From the expressions on their faces, each and every one adored her.

"Hide-and-seek it is."

Colin shot her an incredulous look. How had she gotten hide-and-seek out of those shouts? But no one disagreed. In fact, they all scattered to hide.

One child, a boy of about thirteen, climbed the porch, put his face against the house, curled his arms around his head and began to count.

The air shimmered with excitement. Marlie flashed Colin a smile of pure joy, then skipped down the steps and ran across the lawn.

"Wait!"

She turned and tilted her head.

Why had he stopped her? He'd been alone before, in much scarier places. The war-torn streets of Jerusalem, the bombed-out wreck of Beirut, the crater-racked landscape of Afghanistan. Wind Lake at dusk on an August evening was practically nirvana. So why the sudden sense of panic at the thought of her disappearing into the shadows and leaving him behind?

Marlie took a few steps in his direction. "You can go in and watch *Millionaire*."

"I don't think so."

"Thirty, thirty-one," mumbled the kid who was "it."

"Come on!" Marlie grabbed Colin's hand and yanked him from the porch.

"Kurt is the best seeker in town. You'd better stick with me."

He meant to protest. He certainly didn't want to play. Even if he hadn't been exhausted, he was dressed for a casually elegant dinner, not hide-and-seek.

But the instant she touched him, his jet lag disappeared as energy flowed from her hand through his. He forgot he was waiting for a call from his mother.

He didn't care that he was wearing his best slacks and Italian-leather shoes. What mattered right now was the tangle of their fingers and the way the setting sun caused Marlie's skin to glow like a pearl beneath the endless blue sea.

She zigged through the yard and zagged into the next, cut behind one garage, then between a house and a storage shed. She kept a tight hold on his hand or Colin would have been wandering in the suburban wilderness.

"How far away can we hide?" he asked in a normal tone of voice.

She winced. "Shh!"

"They can't hear me from way over there."

"Ever catch the saying 'Little pitchers have big ears'?"

"Yeah." From his mom, about a thousand times when he was trying to hear something good she and his dad were discussing.

"They do. So keep your lip zipped."

"It's just a game."

She glanced over her shoulder, her face scrunched into a ferocious scowl. "Bite your tongue. Winner of the night's festivities receives a favor of their choice from the loser."

"What kind of favor?"

"In my case, shoveling." She smirked. "These kids are already booked mowing my lawn until the snow flies. If I play my cards right, I won't have to haul snow until well past Easter."

Her mother hustled *Jeopardy!* and Marlie hustled hide-and-seek. He had to admire that.

They reached the last house on the block. "Follow me," she murmured.

Ducking low, she scurried across the lawn, then slipped through a small grove of trees until she reached a weeping willow. "In here."

She dropped to her knees and crawled between the thick hanging branches. He followed.

Being treated to a close-up view of her rear end did little for Colin's interest in the game. It did, however, increase some other interests.

He shook his head. He had to stop thinking of her like that. He wasn't staying — and Marlie was a staying kind of girl.

The foliage fell back where it had been and shadows surrounded them. The space between the willow's branches and the trunk was small — only enough room for them to sit, hip to hip, with their backs against the tree. The ground was damp and turning cool as the sun dipped below the horizon. They were in their own little world.

"Ready or not, here I come!" Kurt shouted, but he seemed far away.

Though the night was quiet, trickles of sound eased into their hiding place. A back door opened with a squeak; a child's name was called before the door closed. Crickets chirped so loudly they almost drowned out the childish voices raised in surprise, which proved that Kurt was indeed a good seeker.

"How long does he have?" Colin whispered.

Marlie leaned in close, her mouth hovering near his ear. "As long as it takes."

Her breast brushed his arm, her breath tickled his neck. He tensed and so did she.

65

She began to move away, but a furtive footstep on the other side of the curtain of branches made them both go still.

"Shh," she breathed, nothing more than a wisp of air.

He nodded and her mouth skimmed his ear. An involuntary gasp escaped. Was it hers or his?

She inched back; the wavering, fading light shining through the branches bounced off her glasses. He couldn't see her eyes, and suddenly he needed to.

Colin slid the hideous things from her nose and found himself lost in brilliant depths of blue.

The footsteps ceased. Were they gone or merely pausing in their quest, waiting for a single, covert murmur?

What had once been merely a game had become something much, much more. Colin's entire body quivered with tension. His ears strained for a hint of sound. He was alive in a way he'd been only a few times before, when his life was at stake, when his entire world was about to change forever.

He wanted to stay beneath the canopy of this tree and inhale the sweet, sugared scent of Marlie. He wanted to touch her skin, bury his face in her hair, hold her close and learn the rhythm of her heart.

He wanted to kiss her, so he did.

Marlie had been holding her breath, trying to hear a whisper or a footstep beyond the willow's branches when Colin removed her glasses, and the world outside ceased to exist.

His gaze wandered over her face. He seemed to like what he saw. Funny, she was without her glasses, yet he couldn't see.

She had no warning, which was lucky because she probably would have made a sound and given their location away. Then she would have missed the best kiss she'd ever had.

Not that she'd had very many. She could count on one hand the times she'd been kissed as a woman should be kissed by a man.

Or perhaps she'd never been kissed the way she should have been, because she had never felt like this. As if she wanted to burrow closer, become a part of him and have him become a part of her. She was drawn to his warmth, captivated by his taste, tantalized by the way he drew her lower lip into his mouth and sucked.

She opened to drink him in, and he deepened the kiss, swallowed her moan.

She forgot where they were, who they were, why they were, lost in the magic of a first embrace.

Marlie wasn't sure where it might have led if several things hadn't happened almost at once.

A cell phone shrilled, so loud she shrieked and leaped away, cracking her head against the trunk of the tree. Marlie saw stars.

The branches of the willow parted and Kurt's face appeared. He said, "Gotcha!" at the same moment Colin said, "Hello?"

Marlie wished for a large and convenient hole that she could crawl into and die.

"Did you find out anything?"

Colin's mother didn't bother with warm and fuzzy greetings. Of course, her son was missing. Not that she'd have bothered with them, anyway. Eleanor Luchetti had never been very warm or fuzzy.

Colin didn't blame her. She'd done the best she could. She only had two hands, one lap, a tenuous hold on sanity.

That all six Luchetti children were productive, even stellar, members of society was a tribute to her mothering abilities. He'd always known she loved him, that he could go to her or his father with any problem and they would help him solve it. That was more than a lot of people could say.

"Not really," he answered, still sitting under the tree.

Marlie crawled out, and Colin was momentarily distracted by her rear end. Lascivious thoughts filled his head and when his mother snapped, "Colin! I am talking to you!" he jumped as if he'd been stuck with a barbecue fork, half-afraid she knew exactly what he'd been thinking. She so often did.

"Uh, sorry, Mom. What was that?"

"I said, did you find out why Bobby sent you to Minnesota?"

The branches of the willow swung shut, obscuring Marlie from his view. Out of sight, out of mind — kind of. At least he wasn't imagining her incredible backside, naked, in just that position, on his bed.

"No," he blurted. "I have no idea why he told me to come here."

Quickly he explained what he did know. The voices of the children came closer, then closer still. He remained shrouded by the willow's branches, his silk pants soaking up all the dampness in the ground.

His mother started to speak, but her words were drowned out by a serenade of barking dogs.

"Silence!" The force of her fury traveled several hundred miles, causing him to snatch the phone away from his ear with a wince.

Tentatively he repositioned the receiver. "You mind? I like my eardrums just the way they are."

"Sorry, but these damned doodles are making me nuts."

Colin assumed the barking was caused by the doodles, but he had no idea what a doodle was. His conversations with his family over the past few months had been mostly about Bobby. Oh, he'd heard the news of Aaron's marriage, his sister's little girl, Dean's plans to adopt a boy named Tim and Evan's constant flitting from one odd job to another.

But doodles? He couldn't recall anything about that.

"John, take those dogs outside and shoot them."

"Aw, Ellie, they love you."

Colin smiled at the calm, sure voice of his dad. John Luchetti was always the quiet amid the chaos. Once, his mom had been, too, until menopause had shortened her fuse to just this side of nonexistent.

"Which only proves they're dumb as dipsticks," she muttered. "Can't stand the little buggers, and they follow me around like I'm their mama."

"I take it that doodles are dogs," Colin said.

She sighed. "Six of them. Make that five. We foisted one off on Aaron."

"You have five dogs?"

Colin found that hard to believe. She hadn't cared for the two they'd had in the first place.

"Seven. We have *seven.* Bear and Bull — plus the result of Bear's little accident with a French poodle."

"Aha! Dalmatian plus poodle equals doodle."

"I never said you weren't as sharp as a needle in a haystack and just as hard to find."

His mom hadn't lost her ability to get in a dig at every opportunity.

"Why don't you give them away?"

"Tell it to your brother."

"Which one?"

"Dean."

Colin frowned. Dean, a natural-born farmer if ever there was one, had never struck him as being overly kind. He was pretty much an equal-opportunity crank. He didn't like anyone and no one liked him. Except for animals — Dean and animals got along just fine. Still, seven dogs was pushing it.

"The kid likes the doodles," Eleanor continued.

"The kid?"

"Tim. The one your niece brought here."

"Zsa Zsa is bringing home boys? Awful precocious for a toddler. Can she even walk yet?"

"Don't be a smart-ass. You have another niece now."

Aaron's girl — the thirteen-year-old daughter of a stripper. He really needed to take a trip home and get a few things straight.

"Anyway, Tim likes the dogs. Dean likes Tim."

"Dean likes someone?"

"You'd be surprised at the changes in Dean since he discovered he's ADHD."

Colin rubbed his forehead. "He's who?"

"Attention deficit hyperactive disorder. It explains quite a few things about your brother."

"Wait a second. When did this happen?"

"Never mind. If you ever get home, you can hear all about it. Right now I want to know what was in Bobby's letters."

Colin's mind stuttered. The letters. Well, duh.

"Colin? What did he write to this girl?"

"I . . . uh, well, I'll let you know."

"You haven't looked at them yet?"

Her incredulous tone only made him more defensive. "It's a little rude to come blazing into town, hit her with Bobby's disappearance, then demand to see her personal correspondence."

"Since when have you cared about being rude?"

True. In his job he had to be aggressive to the point of offensive at times. It had never bothered him, not once. But right now the thought of asking Marlie for his brother's letters made Colin very uncomfortable.

Nevertheless, he had to.

"I'll take care of it," he told his mom.

"When can we expect you?"

"Expect me?"

"Home."

"Who said I was coming home?"

"Where else are you going to go? Do you plan on flying off to Istanbul while we wait to hear if your brother is alive or . . . or . . . ?"

Her voice broke and he gaped. He'd never heard his mother cry. He wasn't sure what to do. He should have known that she would recover on her own. She always did.

"Read the letters," she snapped. "Then get your butt home."

"No."

"No?"

She said the word with the exact same inflection she'd used when he'd been six and refused to eat his peas. And like then, he had the urge to give in and do whatever she asked before she made good on the implied threat in her tone. Unlike then, he didn't.

"I'm staying here."

He hadn't known that until he'd said it. Sure, there was the offer of a room at the Andersons', but he hadn't planned on accepting.

However, when faced with a week on the farm with far too many doodles, the prospect of a little vacation in Minnesota held much more appeal. He could just as easily make phone calls and write e-mails from here as from home. With the added advantage that Bobby might turn up and solve all their problems.

The branches of the willow parted and Marlie's face reappeared. The sight made him remember their kiss. He could still taste her, smell her. The slightly unfocused nature of her gaze made him realize he still held her glasses in his hand. He offered them to her, and she took them with a distracted smile before backing out from under the tree.

"I win," Kurt announced.

"Again! Again!" several others cried.

"Are those children I hear?" Colin started when his mother's voice erupted from his cell phone in a spatter of static.

"Yes."

"What on earth are you doing around children?"

"Playing hide-and-seek."

"You're what?" she said as if he'd admitted to playing a round of naked Twister. Which wasn't a bad idea.

"Is this Colin? Colin Luchetti? The little boy who begged me for no more brothers?"

"Hell, Mom, I had four and a baby sister. You can hardly blame me for being less than excited about kids."

"Hmm. I suppose so. I realize everything that's wrong with my children is my fault."

He rolled his eyes, even though she couldn't see him. Which was lucky. Because rolling of the eyes in the vicinity of his mother often resulted in a good swift smack on the back of his head. He might be a world traveler, respected on five continents, but his mother was still his mother — and she'd knock him into next week if he didn't watch himself.

"There's nothing wrong with me, Mom."

"Of course there isn't. So when did you decide you like children enough to play with them?"

"I didn't. Marlie was playing and I —"

He broke off. He really didn't want to explain to his mother that he'd been enchanted by Marlie Anderson.

"Will you be at the hotel in Wind Lake?"

"There isn't one."

"Oh? Then where . . . ?"

"Mrs. Anderson offered me their extra room upstairs."

"Missus? I thought she was a Miss."

"Marlie lives with her mother."

"Ah."

She meant something by that, but Colin wasn't sure what.

"You're right," she continued. "Stay. Bobby must have had a reason for sending you there. Maybe if you find out what it was, you'll find him."

Colin certainly intended to try.

CHAPTER FIVE

Beneath the excited chatter of the children, Marlie heard the low murmur of Colin's voice. She didn't know what he was saying, but she had heard him refer to the caller as "Mom."

The relief that flooded her at the word was entirely inappropriate. Just because he was talking to his mother now didn't mean he wouldn't be talking to some hot babe in an hour. Colin Luchetti seemed like the kind of man who had a whole entourage of hot babes.

She couldn't care less. She wasn't one of them. Never could be.

"I won, so I want a week off from mowing your lawn," Kurt stated.

Marlie yanked her attention from Colin's voice to the boy in front of her. Since Marlie knew thirteen-year-old males were incapable of subtlety, she concluded that Kurt hadn't seen her and Colin doing the tongue tango. Thank God. How would that sound to the parents of the children in her charge?

"You sure you don't want a hot fudge

sundae every day for a week?" she wheedled. "How about a cheeseburger, fries and a Coke at the café?"

One other thing she knew about teenage boys — they were always hungry.

"Nuh-uh, Miss Marlie. I heard the biggest heat wave of the summer is comin' in on a west wind end of the week."

"It is?"

Late August in Minnesota was the swan song of summer. Nights turned crisp. Days more like autumn than anything else. But sometimes . . . sometimes the west wind blew in more than a storm.

"Sure thing." Kurt nodded so hard he resembled one of those plastic dogs people keep in the back windows of their cars. "I don't want to be mowin' when it's ninety, Miss Marlie."

Neither did she. But fair was fair, and Kurt had won.

"Fine. You're off the hook this week."

"Thanks." He stepped in close and lowered his voice. "You know you can get one of the others to do it easy. Just play Mother May I. You *always* win at that."

Marlie smiled. Kurt was right. However . . . She looked over the assembled throng. The kids here tonight were too young to be mowing her lawn.

A rustle made her turn just as Colin stepped between the branches of the willow. She spun back to the children, her cheeks flaming so badly she feared they must be neon-red. Thankfully no one seemed to notice. Or maybe the night was just too dark.

"Run along home now," she ordered.

"Awwww."

"We can play tomorrow night."

They did as she told them, and Marlie walked out to the street so she could watch every child return safely home. Usually they played more than one game, but tonight Marlie wasn't up to playing more, especially with Colin.

She had no idea why he'd kissed her. He couldn't have wanted to. Was he the kind of man who hit on whatever woman was available just because she was there? He didn't seem like it, but then, what did she know of men?

Nothing. And men like Colin even less.

The idea that the kiss they'd shared, which had been the most exciting of her life, had been to him merely another in a very long line ended her embarrassment, replacing it with annoyance.

She rounded on him. "You brought a cell phone to hide-and-seek?"

He opened his mouth, shut it again. Glanced up at the moon and scratched his head. "Yes?"

"Why?"

"I bring a cell phone everywhere."

Marlie couldn't fathom the need for a cell phone everywhere. But she was sure there were a lot of things about Colin Luchetti she would never be able to fathom.

"We lost," she pointed out.

"I'm sorry."

"Sorry enough to mow my lawn?"

"Sure."

Her mouth fell open. "But . . . I mean, no, that's okay."

"You don't think I can do it? I assure you, I *have* mowed a lawn. Just not lately."

"I mean, it doesn't need to be done until the weekend, and by then you'll be gone."

"I will?"

"You won't?"

"I've decided to stay."

"Where?"

"At your house."

"My what?"

"Your mom said I could. Since I blew our cover and I'm staying in your guest room, it seems only fair that I mow the lawn."

Marlie couldn't get past the news that her mom had offered their spare bedroom to a perfect stranger. Sure, he was Bobby's brother, but heck, she'd never met Bobby. The Luchettis might be a family of handsome serial killers for all she knew.

As if sensing her distress, Colin laid a hand on her shoulder. "If you'd rather I didn't . . ."

The first touch of his fingers and her body sprang to life. The warmth of his skin seeped through her thin cotton shirt. The citrus scent of his aftershave tickled her nose. She remembered how he'd tasted beneath the canopy of the tree, and she knew that no matter how foolish it might be, she had to taste him again.

"No," she murmured. "I'd rather you did."

Lifting her gaze to his, she was captured by what she saw there. A longing equal to her own, memories both new and as old as time.

"Did what?" he whispered.

Me.

The word echoed in her head so loudly Marlie feared she'd said it aloud. She blinked and the moment was gone.

Colin no longer stared at her with undisguised longing. She stepped back. His hand dropped to his side. She started toward home.

"If you want to stay in Wind Lake, you'll *have* to stay with us," she said, proud her voice sounded like her own and not some woman who kissed strange men beneath the willow tree. "There isn't a Hilton anywhere close."

"It's not that I want to . . ." He started after her, then stopped, frustrated. "I mean, I need to. Because of Bobby."

"I see."

Of course he wouldn't *want* to stay. A man like Colin would only want to go.

Marlie seemed sad, and Colin wasn't sure why. Was it the kiss? No woman had ever been sad that he'd kissed her.

But Marlie was unlike any other woman he'd ever known. And that kiss. That kiss had been something special. He wanted to do it again.

She was several feet ahead of him, her pace that of a power walk, not a leisurely stroll. He took a few giant steps and snagged her by the elbow. She was going so fast in one direction that she nearly fell in the other.

He steadied her, enjoying for an instant the creamy softness of her skin, before he reluctantly let her go. "Maybe we should talk."

They stood beneath the harsh white glow of a streetlight — the only one on the block from the looks of things. She tilted her head, and her hair brushed the snout of the purple dinosaur. That dinosaur didn't have it half-bad.

"Talk about what?"

"The kiss."

If they hadn't been standing beneath the bright light, he might not have seen her blush. As it was, the wash of red spread from her neck to her cheeks and settled across her forehead. She ducked and her hair covered her face.

"Hey," he murmured, and reached out to finger the soft strands.

A huge hand clamped on to his wrist, yanking it away from Marlie, then twisting his arm behind his back.

"What kiss?" growled a familiar voice, which Colin couldn't quite place.

"Let him go." Marlie appeared more amused than alarmed.

Colin didn't find the situation funny, especially when his attacker pulled his arm a little higher and he saw black dots in front of his eyes.

"I said, 'What kiss?' "

"None of your business."

This time the pain was sharp enough to make him gasp.

"Garth! Stop being an idiot. He kissed me. Big deal. I'm sure he's kissed a thousand other women. It's not like it meant anything."

Hearing his kiss described in such dismissive terms hurt almost as much as his arm being twisted. Sure he'd kissed other women. Maybe not a thousand. But he liked to think that his kiss had meant something to at least a few of them. Especially to her.

His arm was released so suddenly he almost fell on his face. He hadn't had to fight hand to hand with anyone in a very long time. The Luchetti brothers tried to avoid rolling around in the dirt now that they were over twenty-one.

His weapon these days was the pen — or rather the computer. Which was the only reason anyone had gotten the jump on him. The *only* reason. He was out of practice.

Colin turned and came nose to chest hair with the mammoth cook from the café. The guy appeared angry enough to spit nails — at him.

"Garth, you met Colin. Colin, Garth

Lundquist. My best friend."

Friend? What was with Marlie and her guy friends? He didn't believe for a minute that this one wanted to be just a friend.

"Keep your lips off Marlie," Garth bit out.

Marlie laughed. "Knock it off." She glanced at Colin. "He's just kidding. He likes to be my big, bad protector." She slid between them and patted Garth's massive chest.

Garth never took his gaze from Colin's. Colin returned the favor. They stared at each other like two dogs with a single, juicy bone.

"What's the matter with you?" Marlie pushed an ineffectual hand against the Viking invader. He didn't move an inch.

"I don't care whose brother you are. You can't just come into town and start seducing the schoolteachers."

"Garth!" Marlie squeaked. "Have you lost your mind?"

He picked her up by the elbows and set her to the side. She sputtered and mumbled as the man stepped in close to Colin and pushed a finger the size of a bratwurst into his chest. It hurt almost as much as the arm twisting had.

"Never touch her again."

"It was an accident."

"There had better not be any more accidents or I'll accidentally rearrange your face. Got it?"

Colin shrugged, hoping the noncommittal movement would be enough. He wasn't going to agree to anything of the sort, but he didn't want to die under the only street lamp in the smallest town west of the Mississippi. If he had to go, he planned to do so in a blaze of glory in an exotic foreign land.

Sadly, Garth wasn't as dumb as he looked. "What was that?" he said, tilting his ear in Colin's direction. "I didn't hear anything."

Colin sighed, opened his mouth to tell Garth where he could shove his orders, and Marlie interrupted. "Big Jake! Garth, it's *Jake.*"

The man immediately stepped away from Colin, letting his arm fall back to his side. Colin rubbed the spot Garth had been poking. There'd be a bruise there tomorrow.

He'd gotten off lucky. If he'd opened his mouth, Garth would have wiped the street with his face. Marlie might insist her "best friend" was kidding, but Colin, and Garth, knew better.

They all turned to stare at the little boy on the sidewalk. How long had he been there? Long enough, from the scowl he aimed Colin's way.

"Hi, Jake," Colin said.

"Ned don't like you," Jake informed him. His bottom lip shot out. "So I don't, neither."

"Either," Marlie corrected. "I mean . . . Jake, that's not nice. Mr. Luchetti is a guest."

Jake didn't seem to care. He narrowed his eyes, took his dad's hand and tugged. "Ned wants to watch *America's Most Wanted*. He says there's too many strangers in town. One of 'em might be a fugital."

"Fugitive," Marlie said, then pressed her fingers to her forehead. "Never mind. Good night, you two."

She turned and walked toward her house. Garth's huge hand landed on Colin's shoulder. "Where do you think you're going?"

"I'm staying with the Andersons."

Garth's fingers clenched. "What?"

Colin winced. "Mrs. Anderson invited me."

"Marlie, are you crazy?"

"Not *me*," she muttered, and kept on walking.

Colin managed to extricate himself from Garth's grip and hurried after her. He stopped at the car and retrieved his bag and laptop from the trunk. When he glanced back at the Lundquists, father and son stared at him with identical expressions of frustrated fury.

He couldn't blame them. He'd only known Marlie a day and he wanted to protect her forever. How must Garth and Jake feel, having known her all of their lives?

Marlie walked into the house, her mind still outside with Garth. What had gotten into him?

"Martin?" her mother called.

Marlie tamped down the urge to tell her mother that Martin Anderson would never walk in the door again. It wouldn't do any good. Besides, she really didn't want to continue the same old argument with Colin breathing down her neck.

She glanced over her shoulder. He didn't appear upset over Garth's verbal threats and physical intimidation. In Wind Lake, when Garth got annoyed, people got out of his way. Colin hadn't seemed frightened in the least. She'd thought he was smarter than that.

"Oh, it's you, dear." Julie barely glanced

up from *The Match Game* as Marlie came into the room.

"Colin's decided to stay upstairs."

"Fine." Her mother waved a hand at the ceiling. "Everything he needs is there."

"I appreciate the room, Mrs. Anderson." Colin lounged in the doorway.

"Stay as long as you like."

"Thank you. I will. Good night."

He appeared so suave and cool — until he turned around and revealed the mud stain across the seat of his slacks.

"Oh, no!" Marlie cried.

"What?"

"Your pants are ruined."

He twisted, grimaced and then shrugged. "I've got others."

Of course he did. He probably threw out his slacks, rather than going through the hassle of getting them dry-cleaned.

"I'll show him the room," Marlie said.

Julie was too busy tsking at the television to care. "That Gene Rayburn. In this day and age he'd be sued for sexual harassment."

"I doubt it," Marlie muttered.

Her mom had never been out of Wind Lake. Heck, she hadn't been out of the house in the past five years. Julie had no idea what the world was like. What had been risqué in the 1970s was a joke in the twenty-first century.

Still, Marlie would have to watch herself. Folks might be used to a lot more sex on television, but in Wind Lake they wouldn't put up with their preschool teacher making whoopee with a stranger — even if it was under her own mother's roof.

Marlie cleared her throat and hopefully her mind. What was the matter with her? They'd shared one kiss and suddenly she was having an affair? Foolish, since Colin hadn't seemed interested in kissing her again. When Garth had given him the ultimatum, he'd shrugged.

Then he'd had the nerve to refer to their embrace as an accident. An accident? As if their lips had collided, then his tongue had fallen into her mouth?

Marlie stomped into the hallway. She yanked open the door that housed the staircase and thumped up the stairs. Colin was right behind her.

"Full bath." She jabbed a thumb at the first door on the right. "Empty room." Her index finger flicked to the left. "Bedroom." She opened the last door near the back of the house and hit the lights.

Twin beds covered with discarded comforters from her youth dominated the room. A nightstand with a reading lamp was between them, and an old dresser had been shoved against the near wall.

She swept out her arm. "Here you go. The Wind Lake Hilton."

Colin hesitated, his gaze shifting back and forth between the two beds.

"Something wrong?" she asked.

"I can't decide if I want to sleep with Bert and Ernie or Barbie."

"That sounds obscene."

"It does, doesn't it?"

"I can change the bedding. Maybe. I'm not sure if we have anything else. How about if I switch mine with yours? I don't mind Bert and Ernie."

"You have a single bed?"

"Sure. Why not?"

He shook his head. "Seems small."

"Why, when there's only me in it?"

Forever and ever.

"What about Bert and Ernie?"

"They like to share."

"I've heard that about them." He smiled. "Never mind. The bedding is fine. Although you may hear a thump or two in the night when I fall on the floor. I'm not used to a single."

"I just bet you aren't."

Silence followed her comment and she

wanted to take it back. Who he slept with was none of her business.

"You don't like me much, do you?"

On the contrary, she liked him a lot. Perhaps too much.

"I don't even know you."

"We could change that. I'm going to be here awhile."

"How long?"

"As long as it takes to find Bobby."

Bobby. She hadn't thought of him in hours. How could she be so selfish, contemplating kisses and sheets and Colin sleeping with beautiful, thin, other women?

"What are you going to do?"

"He sent me here for a reason. Maybe if I can figure out what that was, I'll find him. Do you still have his letters?"

"Of course."

Tied with a ribbon and hidden in her lingerie drawer, such that it was — a black lace slip she'd ordered from Victoria's Secret on a whim and a hot-pink garter one of the kids had given her for Valentine's Day because it was "pwetty."

"May I see them?" Her eyes flicked to his. "Please?"

There was nothing in those letters that couldn't be read by anyone in town. So why did she hesitate?

Because they were hers. The only correspondence she'd ever had with a man. The only man she'd ever known who hadn't been from Wind Lake — until this one had walked into her life.

None of that mattered. Even if the letters had been passionate missives that defined a love for all time, she would have let Colin read them. Because she'd do anything to help find Bobby.

"I'll get them," she said, and slipped from the room.

Colin listened to Marlie's footsteps as she descended the staircase. He set his things next to the wall. A low murmur as she spoke to her mother drifted upward. His mind meandered back to his life on the farm.

Every night he would listen to the rise and fall of his parents' voices downstairs. At precisely ten o'clock John and Ellie would walk up the steps together. The heavy thud of his father's work boots hitting the wall in the next room signaled an end to the day.

The procedure never wavered. As boring as Colin had believed that to be when he was fifteen, he now understood he'd been given a charmed childhood. There had never been a single night when his parents had not walked up the steps and slept only a shout away.

Colin had shared a bedroom with Bobby. Oh, how he'd moaned and groaned about that. Kim, their sister — the Princess, as Dean liked to call her — had her own room. But really, what was she supposed to do — bunk with one of the boys?

Still they'd all razzed her for being the anointed one. None of them had discovered until recently how tough her life had been.

Dean had shared with Evan and Aaron. Which was probably why, despite Dean's disposition, there were rarely any fights in their room. Aaron had no doubt dispelled all the conflicts before they could get out of hand, with his tranquil manner and serene voice.

Their big brother was a saint in farmer's clothing. Or at least he'd tried to be. No one ever understood why Aaron had dropped out of college after one year, leaving his dreams of the priesthood behind him.

Until recently, anyway, when his daughter had shown up on the doorstep. Colin would have liked to have been there for that.

As kids, he and Bobby had fought over

everything. His brother supported the government; Colin knew they were up to something. Colin studied hard so he could get a scholarship; Bobby lifted weights so he could join the army. Colin dreamed of writing about exotic foreign lands; Bobby dreamed of kicking slimy foreign ass.

At one point they'd drawn a line in Magic Marker right down the center of their room, each vowing to stay on their side. That had worked pretty well until their mom walked in. They'd spent the following Friday night repainting the wall and all day Saturday scrubbing the floor. They'd never completely erased that line, and their mother had never let them forget it.

But no matter how much they fought, no matter what they'd said or done to each other that day, when the lights went off and they lay in their bunk beds, they talked about everything — girls and school, dreams and hopes, secrets and fears.

Nothing they said to each other in that room ever went any further. When the stars came out and the crickets chirped or the coyotes yowled, all was forgiven, forgotten because they were friends, confidants, brothers.

"I *will* find you," Colin vowed to the empty room.

Footsteps sounded on the staircase again. He already knew Marlie's stride. She jogged up the steps with an easy, light-footed gait, and seconds later she entered the room, her hands full of envelopes.

"How many are there?"

"Maybe twenty?"

"Twenty? In less than a year?"

Pink spread across her cheeks. "Is that a lot?"

For Bobby, he'd have to say yes. Wasn't the guy busy keeping the world safe? He had time to write a girl twenty times?

Hell, Colin was a writer and *he* didn't write letters. That was why they'd invented e-mail. Which reminded him . . .

"You don't have e-mail?"

"Me? What for?"

"Cheaper than letters."

"I have no friends or relatives outside of Wind Lake."

"None?"

"Except for Bobby. He said he'd rather write letters. He never knew when he'd get near a computer."

"Uh-huh."

Colin suspected that any e-mail from U.S. Special Forces stationed in hellholes around the world was censored — or at least read by beady-eyed trolls kept in secure bunkers beneath the Mojave Desert. No wonder Bobby had preferred snail mail — not that Colin wouldn't put it past the trolls to search through that, too.

"Well, thanks." Colin held out his hand.

Marlie's fingers clenched on the envelopes. "I doubt these will help you. There's hardly anything personal in them, and I know there's nothing that would tell us where he might be."

"Maybe not. But I still need to look."

"All right." She released the letters and inched toward the door. "I have to go. My mother wants me to play *$10,000 Pyramid* with her and Donny."

"Donny?"

"Osmond. The new host."

"Oh." Their habit of talking about game-show personalities as if they lived and breathed in Wind Lake was a bit disconcerting.

"Good night," she whispered, and escaped before he could reply.

Colin tossed the letters onto the Barbie bed and crossed the room to open a window. Fresh, cool air poured in, along with the noises of the night. A car passed by, the *whoosh* of its tires blending with the rustle of the breeze through the trees in the yard. A dog barked to the west, another

97

answered to the east, and somewhere on the block a baby cried.

Different sounds from the ones he was used to. On the farm their nearest neighbor lived several miles away. Night noises consisted of cows mooing, pigs snuffling, a coyote calling from the creek bed. Those were the memories of his youth.

Over the past several years he'd learned to ignore the rumble of traffic, the roaring of sirens, even the rattle of gunfire. Not that he didn't like big cities. He did. But places with thousands, millions of people were loud — there was no help for it. He no longer left his window open when he slept — suicidal he wasn't. Tonight, however, he could sleep as he had when he was a boy, with a breeze to cool his skin and peace to soothe his soul.

Colin shucked his ruined slacks and tossed them into the trash. Then he dug out the ragged shorts and T-shirt he slept in before settling down with Bert and Ernie to read his brother's letters.

An hour later he threw the last one on top of the pile. Dated the week before Bobby had gone missing, it gave no more hint than any of the others where his brother might be.

Marlie was right — Bobby had written virtually nothing about his current situation. Probably because he couldn't. He'd told stories about his childhood, the farm, talked to her about his family. No wonder Colin felt as if Marlie knew him. His brother had introduced him long ago.

Despite the lack of information, Colin *had* learned something useful — the reason Bobby had sent him here.

Someday I hope we can meet so I can tell you in person what a great girl you are. You're the best thing that ever happened to me, Marlie.

Colin got up and walked to the window. He leaned down and let the wind cool his face. He'd been right to follow his instinct and stay here. Sooner or later here was where his brother would come.

Because Bobby was head-over-heels crazy for Marlie Anderson.

CHAPTER SIX

Colin tossed and turned most of the night. He couldn't believe he'd kissed his brother's girl. Such things weren't done in the Luchetti family. They might steal each other's shirts, borrow each other's money, kick each other's ass, but they never, ever touched another's girl.

Of course he hadn't known she was Bobby's. How was he supposed to when she didn't even know it herself?

The cryptic note made a certain kind of sense in light of this new development. Bobby cared for Marlie. But did he want Colin to watch over her until he returned? Or take care of her if he could not?

These questions, and many more, kept Colin awake well past 3:00 a.m. When he finally fell asleep, his dreams were tangled, troubled. He slept late and awoke more tired than he'd been in the first place.

The scent of coffee greeted him as he opened the door to the first floor.

"Grab a cup and a muffin. You're just in time for *The Price is Right*," Mrs. Anderson called from the living room.

Colin did as he was told, biting into the best blueberry muffin he'd ever had, then washing it down with coffee that would rival any he'd sipped in European cafés.

"Wrong!" Mrs. Anderson threw a pillow at the television set. "What idiot thinks a washer and dryer sells for three hundred dollars?"

"Um, that idiot?" Colin contemplated the insane woman trying to strangle Bob Barker.

"No. She won. The idiot is still down on the floor with the others."

"Ah." Colin nodded sagely, though he didn't understand.

"Is Marlie here?" he asked during the commercial break. He wanted to talk to her about the letters, his brother, and maybe slip in an apology for his own behavior while he was at it.

Mrs. Anderson checked her watch. "It's 10:00 a.m."

Colin opened his mouth, then shut it again. Marlie said her mom had all her marbles, but sometimes he wondered. He hadn't *asked* what time it was.

Nevertheless, he said, "Thank you."

Mrs. Anderson looked at him as if he was the one without any marbles. "She's been at work for four hours already."

"But last night she didn't get home until five-thirty."

"Last night was a good night."

Sometimes Colin worked for days, even weeks, at a time, hiked up mountains, slept in ditches, dodged bullets, wrote copy until dawn to make a deadline, but that was nothing when compared to twelve hours alone with all those children.

"Doesn't she have any help?"

"Most days one of the students from the high school comes in at three. Then Marlie can do her paperwork while someone else takes care of the children."

Whoopee, he wanted to say. Confined to the office with her rat-thing, filling out forms in triplicate while a teenager asked her a question every other minute. Colin shook his head. The woman was a saint.

"What about lunch?" he asked.

Mrs. Anderson smiled and patted his knee. "Don't worry, honey, I'll make lunch, too. I heard boys are big eaters, but since I never had any of my own, I didn't realize they worried about lunch while they were still eating breakfast."

"No, I didn't mean —" He broke off. "I wanted to know what Marlie did for lunch."

"Oh. Well, she eats with the children, if

she has the time. Poor thing, I worry that she doesn't get her vitamins."

"Maybe I should take her something. Make sure she eats right at least today."

Mrs. Anderson beamed. "I'll pack you a basket."

While she did that, he went upstairs to check his messages. His employer had left a terse, "Call me," so Colin did.

"I need you in North Korea yesterday."

His boss, Geraldine Stratton, had a lot in common with his mother. She rarely bothered with a greeting, on the phone or in person. She always expected more from him — no matter what he did — and she ran her kingdom with an iron hand.

Gerry came from a family of newsmen. Her father was a correspondent in the Pacific, her grandfather had covered the Great War. Hell, she probably had relatives who'd ridden up San Juan Hill with Teddy or crouched in a trench near Shiloh.

But much to her father's dismay, his only child had been a girl. That didn't mean she didn't have newsprint in her veins. She just hadn't been of an era when women went to war. Poor Gerry had been born about twenty years too early.

Still, she was the best at her job, one of the reasons Colin stayed with the *Dispatch* even though he could have taken a position in a bigger city or hired himself out to the highest bidder.

"I'm on vacation," he reminded her.

"You never go on vacation."

"All the more reason I should."

"Where are you?"

He'd told her, but while Gerry's mind was a steel trap for information about politics and crime, minor tidbits such as where her foreign correspondent had gone slipped through her brain like water through a rusty bucket.

She would not appreciate the analogy, but Colin did.

"Minnesota," he answered.

"What did Jesse Ventura do now? And why do you care? You're a *foreign* correspondent."

"I'm miles away from Jesse."

Which is just the way I like it, he thought.

"Colin, I need you to hop a plane for Pyongyang."

"Can't."

"Can't or won't?"

"What difference does it make? I'm not going."

"What could you possibly be working on that's more important than this?"

For Gerry, life was work, work was life and nothing else mattered. He was usually right behind her.

"I'm working on finding my brother. I don't give a rat's ass about North Korea."

"Haven't you been watching the news? There's trouble."

"There's always trouble. It can get in line."

Silence met his statement. Colin rubbed his forehead. On any other given day, he'd be thrilled to head for Pyongyang. Though communism's big experiment had failed on many fronts, there was still North Korea, China and, of course, that nut in Cuba to contend with. Colin's job security was never in question. He enjoyed being where the action was. He thrived on it.

But he couldn't leave Wind Lake. Not now. The very thought made his gut clench and his senses scream an alert. He was enough of a newsman to know that a hunch had to be followed, and his hunch said he had to stay here.

"Send someone else," he told his boss. "I've got a responsibility to my brother."

"You could be missing the story of the century."

"It's awful early in the century for that, don't you think?"

Gerry sighed. "Fine. But you can't tell me that you won't be bored in Montana within a week."

"Minnesota," he corrected.

"Whatever. When you call begging for an assignment, there may not be any pending disasters left."

"Right. Like that'll happen."

He could have sworn he heard a laugh, quickly stifled. However, when Gerry spoke again, there was not a hint of humor in her voice. "Don't be gone too long, Luchetti. The news business moves fast. You get behind, I'm not waiting up."

She clicked off without a goodbye. Gerry didn't believe in niceties on either end of a conversation.

He experienced a moment of unease at the plum assignment he'd just given up. There was no doubt something brewing in North Korea. There always was.

Gerry's threat of losing any headway he'd made in his career also stung. But if he couldn't take a week's vacation once in a while, what was the reason for working so hard in the first place?

The idea was so novel, so unexpected, so unlike him, Colin stood in the middle of the room scratching his head. One day in Godforsaken, Minnesota, and he was already thinking strange thoughts.

"Colin?" Mrs. Anderson called.

Colin hurried to the top of the steps. "Yes, ma'am."

"You can call me Julie. I have your lunch packed and sitting by the door. I need to get back to Chuck."

"Norris?"

"Barris. *The Gong Show*? Did you know he was a hit man for the CIA?" She shook her head. "I suppose no one would ever suspect a silly man like that of being an assassin."

She disappeared, leaving Colin completely confused. Sometimes he wasn't altogether sure Julie should be left alone.

He glanced at his watch. Nearly eleven o'clock. He still had time to call his mother, if he was quick about it. But when he did, all he got was the machine again, so he left another message.

"I read the letters and I . . ."

He didn't think he should tell her that Bobby was in love with Marlie. What good would that do? His mother would want to come to Minnesota and meet her, and he didn't want Marlie to know about Bobby's feelings. Not yet. Not when Bobby might very well be dead.

"There was nothing in them of any

help," he finished. "I'll get back to you if I find out anything new."

He ended the call, considered turning off the phone and rejected the idea. While he might not want to talk to Gerry, he did want to talk to Bobby or anyone who'd heard from him. From now until this situation was resolved, Colin would leave his cell phone on. Even if it did ruin a good game of hide-and-seek.

Marlie had slept well. Amazingly so, considering what had happened. The kiss, the argument, Colin's presence directly above her. When she awoke at five o'clock, ten minutes before her alarm was set to erupt, she reached over and shut the thing off.

No matter when she went to bed or how tired she was, Marlie always awoke promptly at 5:00 a.m., even on the weekends. It was a curse.

Or maybe a blessing. Her favorite time of the week was Saturday, when she could enjoy her coffee and a book in the living room alone, without the blare of a game show to mar her peace.

However, when she awoke that morning, every dream she'd had the whole night flooded back. She'd dreamed of Colin —

in ways she'd never dreamed of anyone else.

So when he walked into Chasing Rainbows just before lunch, Marlie's face flushed before he even said a word.

He wore a pair of light-gray slacks and a black shirt that screamed for a tie. He'd left the top two buttons open, hinting at a casualness not reflected in the spit shine of his black leather shoes. The picnic basket in his hand looked severely out of place.

"Your mother sent lunch."

"I'm surprised she could tear herself away from . . ." Marlie's mind blanked.

"Chuck," he supplied with a grin. "Barris, not Norris. Something about a gong and the CIA."

"Ah, Retro Thursday. At least she'll be occupied with reruns for the rest of the day. The Game Show Channel has saved my life."

"Now that's a phrase I don't hear every day."

Even though the sight of him brought back heated memories of her dreams, Marlie couldn't help but smile. Having Colin in Wind Lake, in her house, in her life, might be the most exciting thing that had ever happened to her.

And wasn't that pathetic?

"What's *he* doin' here?" Jake stared at Colin with a ferocious scowl.

"Be nice, Big Jake. Mr. Luchetti brought me lunch."

"She can have my lunch. Go away."

Colin raised a brow but he didn't say a word. Which was just as well. She doubted anything he could say would appease Jake right now. For some reason Jake and his father had taken a dislike to Colin. She'd deal with the son now. Garth, she would deal with later.

"Jake," she said in a warning tone. "Remember what I told you the first day you came to school?"

His sweet face scrunched together with the effort of his thoughts. "Uh, just 'cuz we don't like someone don't mean we can be mean to 'em?"

"Something like that."

Actually, she'd said he should keep an open mind and give everyone a chance. Still, Jake didn't have too many friends — besides Ned. Perhaps this was the reason. He was jealous when his friends made new ones. With Ned, he never had that problem.

"Okay." He dug the toe of his sneaker into the carpet. "I'll try to be nice, but it won't be easy."

"You liked Mr. Luchetti yesterday."

"That was before he started kissin' on you."

Marlie choked. She hadn't realized Jake had heard that part of the conversation.

She glanced around the room. The other children were engrossed in play, some making a sand castle in the sand pit near the window, others putting the letters of the alphabet into their proper order on a magnetic blackboard.

A few of the girls, each dressed like a mini-fashion model, were having a tea party with a cavalcade of teddy bears. Marlie had learned her first week as a teacher that little girls received so many clothes as gifts they had no choice but to wear lace and velvet to preschool. Where else did a four-year-old go?

Thankfully none of the children appeared to have heard Jake's statement.

"Never mind that," Marlie admonished him. "Can you find Houdini for me?"

"Sure." Jake ran off, but not before giving Colin the evil eye.

"Sorry," she said.

"It's all right. If I had a teacher like you, I wouldn't want some strange guy kissing on her, either."

Her cheeks flamed. Marlie hated being a

blue-eyed blonde. Every minor embarrassment played out all over her face.

"Could we forget about last night?" she whispered, casting a glance at the children.

"I'd like to apologize."

Great. He was sorry he'd kissed her. Probably because she was such a sorry kisser.

"I shouldn't have done it," he added.

Shouldn't? Why? Because he didn't really want to? Or because there was someone else?

The cuckoo clock sounded the hour. As if programmed — and they were — the children put away their things and retrieved their lunches.

"Excuse me." Marlie hurried to open juice, milk and stubborn plastic containers. When she turned, Colin was no longer there. A shadow moving in her office revealed where he had gone.

A half hour later, she supervised the bathroom line, then got the children settled for a nap. Jake reported Houdini still MIA, which was nothing new. The guinea pig must have at least a dozen secret hiding places in her office alone.

Two stories, several hugs, a few back rubs, and they were all quiet. For how long was anyone's guess.

Most days while the children napped, Marlie returned phone calls, ordered supplies and straightened up the areas of the school where the children weren't sleeping. Sometimes she ate lunch at her desk; most days she didn't eat lunch at all. She thought about the mountain of work that awaited her, the work she wouldn't get done today, and she got a little dizzy.

But when she stepped into the room, all thoughts of work fled. Colin had put a tablecloth in the center of the floor, placed the food on top. Then he must have lain down to wait for her — and fallen asleep. There was no telling when Houdini had decided to crawl on to Colin's chest for a nap of his own.

CHAPTER SEVEN

Marlie tiptoed across the room, hoping to snatch Houdini before either one knew what hit them. But the guinea pig was an old hand at the art of escape.

She was just reaching for him — slowly, she thought silently — when his little brown head went up, his little pink nose twitched and he raced for freedom, straight across Colin's face.

Colin's eyes shot open. The guinea pig's legs scrambled for purchase in his hair. He opened his mouth to howl and Marlie clapped her hand over his lips.

"Shh. You'll scare him."

Houdini made a mighty leap from Colin's head and kept on running. She doubted they'd see him for at least a day.

Marlie removed her hand. Colin sat up and brushed frantically at his hair, making disgusted noises all the while. She had a hard time not laughing.

"Scare him?" He gave her an incredulous stare. "Scare *him?* My heart's beating two hundred times a minute."

"He likes you."

"I don't like him."

"I got that. But why?"

"I have an aversion to rats. A lot of people do."

"Houdini isn't a rat."

"Tell it to my adrenal glands." Colin reached for a baby carrot and crunched the vegetable with gusto.

"I've never seen a man so afraid of a rodent."

He swallowed. "Just because I'm a guy I'm supposed to like them?"

"Well, at least not be scared of them."

"Isn't that a little sexist?"

She tilted her head and considered. "I suppose so."

"My sister was always scared of mice. Probably because my brothers tormented her with them. You should hear her scream whenever she sees one." He smiled with obvious affection. "I bet she's screaming a lot since she became a farmer's wife."

"Mice never bothered me," Marlie said.

"They never bothered my mom, either. She used to pick them up by their tails and fling them out the door."

Marlie wasn't sure she'd go that far, but she certainly wouldn't scream if she saw a little ol' mouse. "So you don't know why you're scared of rats?"

"I need a reason?" He offered her a choice of sandwich — tuna or PB and J. She took the tuna.

"I guess not. An irrational fear needs no reason, hence —"

"Its irrationality."

"Bingo." Marlie took a bite of her sandwich, washed it down with a swig from her juice box. She loved those things. Juice in a box — modern technology at its finest.

Colin gave her a slice of pineapple. "The rats I've come across in other countries are so big and so numerous . . . They creep me out."

A skittering sound from behind the desk made him jump to his feet. Warily, he eyed the floor. "Uh, do you mind if I sit on a chair?"

She couldn't help but smile. His aversion to Houdini was . . . cute. Though she doubted he'd think so. She wanted to hold him close and keep him safe. She doubted he'd approve of that thought, either.

"I should get off the floor myself." Marlie stood and grabbed two folding chairs that were leaning against the wall. "I'm not as young as I used to be."

"You and me, both." Colin unfolded the chairs and offered one to her.

"If there are so many rats in underdeveloped countries . . ." Marlie's voice trailed off.

"How can I do my job?"

"Well, yeah."

"Sometimes it isn't easy. But I'm not going to let an irrational fear cheat me out of my dream."

"Being a reporter?"

He nodded. "That's all I've ever wanted to be."

"Why?" Marlie had always been fascinated with the reasons people had for becoming who they were. Sometimes there wasn't much of a reason at all, just a series of accidental events.

"When I was a kid, I shoveled manure, milked cows, fed pigs. I couldn't wait to get out. At night I studied pictures of places in books, and I dreamed of seeing every one. I read about people and I wanted to meet them, talk to them, learn about them."

Though she didn't understand the interest, the passion in his voice, on his face, captivated her. Marlie had never wanted to go anywhere but Wind Lake, never been interested in anyone other than the people who lived there. For someone to dream of putting their life on the line just to see foreign places and meet new people was beyond her comprehension, and she said so.

He spread his hands. "I can't understand never wanting to leave home. I went to college and I didn't come back."

"Ever?"

"For a few days now and then. Holidays mostly. In the summers I got internships at newspapers. I was a glorified gofer, but I learned a lot from hanging around and listening to the newspeople talk."

"You enjoy writing?"

He shrugged. "It's a means to an end."

"What end?"

"I want to see the world, learn about it, and I want to relate what I've seen and learned to as many people as I can. If we understand each other, then maybe we won't be fighting all the time."

Marlie couldn't imagine the Israelis and the Palestinians getting along. Holy land was holy land, and neither side would ever give it up or learn to share.

"You *are* a dreamer."

"Never said I wasn't." Colin finished his sandwich. "Someday I want to be as famous as Ernie Pyle."

"Who?"

He gaped. "You can't be serious. Ernie Pyle? The most famous war correspondent in history. He reported on D day and the liberation of Paris, won a Pulitzer. Then he went on to cover the war in the Pacific and was killed by a Japanese sniper."

"Never heard of him," she admitted. "Then again, I don't hear much about anyone famous except Dick Clark and Monty Hall." Marlie studied Colin for a minute. "I thought you wanted to change the world. Suddenly you want to be famous?"

"You can't have one without the other."

He was a mystery. One she'd love to learn more about. They might be as different as north and south, but he still fascinated her. Or maybe it was the differences that drew her to him.

"I read Bobby's letters."

Marlie, who'd been packing the leftovers back into the picnic basket, glanced up. Colin tossed the trash into the garbage can next to her desk.

"And?"

"I didn't find any clues as to where he might be."

"I didn't think you would."

"I do have a few questions."

Marlie snapped shut the lid on the picnic basket. "Ask away, but be quick. Sooner or later one of them's going to wake up, and then they all will."

"You gave me every one of his letters?"

"Of course." Marlie frowned. "Why?"

"I just thought . . . There was nothing . . . I guess I hoped for more."

"I'm sorry there wasn't."

"Bobby was — *is* — the sharpest knife in the Luchetti drawer — except for our sister." Colin shook his head. "He could have had an academic scholarship, but he chose to enlist. If that wasn't enough, he volunteered for Special Forces training. Went to college at night to earn the required degree and spent a year learning freaking Arabic. I never understood him."

"He's committed to protect and serve. Thank goodness there are a few Bobbys out there, or our police and armed forces would be mighty small."

"I wish he were a cop. At least he wouldn't be dismantling nuclear weapons and assassinating terrorists. Much."

Marlie's eyes widened. "Is that what he does?"

"No. Maybe. I don't know. He doesn't tell me anything. Can't really, and that's all right, because if I knew the truth, I'd only worry more."

From the expression on his face, Colin already worried plenty. That he loved his brother so much made her heart soften further.

Marlie reached out. "He'll be all right. If anyone could be, that someone would be Bobby Luchetti."

His hand turned and he twined his fingers with hers. Marlie's stomach quivered, and she forgot how to breathe. How could a single, innocent touch make her feel so many not-very-innocent things?

"I just miss him," Colin murmured.

Marlie blinked. She might be lost in sensation, seduced by his touch, but he was still focused on Bobby — as she should be. She was a deprived virgin lusting after James Bond, and she needed to remember that.

Marlie withdrew her hand from his.

He made an impatient sound. "I'm no better off than I was when I started."

"That's not true. You know there's no cryptic code in my letters."

"We may never find him," Colin murmured.

Marlie wanted to deny that, but she couldn't. Instead, she took Colin's hand again, and this time she didn't let go.

Colin couldn't remember the last time he'd held hands with a woman.

Oh, he'd held hands — with *girls* in

high school. But since then? He couldn't remember doing so, and that was sad. Because holding hands with Marlie was one of the best times he'd ever had.

She knew how to comfort with just a touch. She'd no doubt gotten a lot of practice — cut knees, bruised elbows, bumped heads. If he told her where it hurt, would she kiss it and make it better? He was tempted to find out.

But then, she'd been tempting him since he got here. He had to remember his brother loved her, and that made Marlie Anderson off-limits.

"You'll find Bobby." She squeezed his hand. "I know you will."

"I'm glad you have confidence."

"You don't?"

He wanted to reassure her, but he couldn't lie. Not to that face.

"If the army lost him, I doubt I can get him back."

"But you're going to try, right?"

"Yeah. I'm going to try."

"How?"

Damn good question.

"I'll call in every favor I'm owed, promise anyone, anything, contact every person I've ever met if I have to."

"Where?"

"Iraq, Iran, Israel. New York, L.A., Chicago." He shrugged. "He could be anywhere."

Or nowhere, his mind whispered. Colin ignored his mind. But from the expression on Marlie's face, she'd read it, anyway.

"You don't think it'll do any good, do you?"

"I'm not sure. But I'm not going to give up and bury him without a fight. He'd do the same for me. The second I get a lead, I'll be on a plane."

"What if the lead is in Yemen?"

"What if it is? I've been there before."

Her eyes widened. "You have?"

"Ten times."

"It's so dangerous."

He rubbed his thumb along the back of her hand. "There are places a lot more dangerous than Yemen. And if Bobby's in one, I'll be there tomorrow."

Silence descended, broken only by a slight scratching from behind the file cabinet. Colin ignored that, too.

"It must be nice having a brother."

"Nice?" Colin's thumb froze at the base of hers. "Not exactly."

"I always wanted an older brother, a younger sister."

"But there was just you."

"Yeah. I read a lot. Watched TV. Played solitaire."

Colin thought back to the wrestling matches, games of tag, footraces, football tournaments. While he'd been complaining about never being alone for a minute, he'd never considered what it might be like to be alone all the time. No wonder Marlie played night games with the children.

"What was it like?" she asked, echoing his thoughts.

"To have brothers?"

"Uh-huh."

"Loud. Irritating. Fun." He thought a minute. "Loud."

She laughed. "So it was loud?"

"My mom used to say our volume control had been broken at birth."

"What about your sister?"

"She used to say we'd all been dropped on our heads." He smiled. "We tormented her unmercifully. But we loved her, too. No one touched Kimmy when we were around."

Except for Brian Riley, and he'd done a lot more than touch her. He'd gotten her pregnant — twice. Luckily Dean had already kicked Brian's ass. Eight years after the first infraction, true, but there was no statute of limitations on impregnating little sisters.

Since Brian and Kim were now happily married, Colin doubted he'd be allowed to beat the crap out of Brian anytime soon, no matter how much he might want to.

Marlie's sigh held both sadness and longing. The sound made his chest catch. Colin wanted to comfort her, but he didn't know how.

His mom had never been much of a cuddler. She hadn't had the time. When one of them got hurt, they were told, *Suck it up. Rub a little dirt on it. Quit being a sissy.* Or any one of the other sayings used to make men out of boys. As a result, softer moments had been few and far between in the Luchetti household. At a loss, Colin squeezed Marlie's hand as she had squeezed his.

He must have done something right, because she rewarded him with a dazzling smile, and suddenly he couldn't think straight.

Obviously, because if he'd been thinking, he wouldn't have drawn her forward, leaned in close, caught the scent of pineapple on her lips and honey in her hair.

If he'd had a single cell left firing in his brain, he wouldn't have let his mouth wander over her forehead, across her eyebrow, then down to her cheek. He wouldn't have slid his hand from her wrist to her elbow and contemplated pulling her into his lap for more than a nibble.

Her sigh was no longer sad, but it was still filled with longing, tugging at him in places never visited by a woman's sigh, places never touched by another human soul. Places that were Colin's alone, and now they were hers.

Though he'd sworn never to kiss her again, that vow was lost in the torrent of emotions that ripped through him in the wake of her sigh. His mouth drifted lower, his hands inched higher. Their breath mingled and she gagged.

Colin's eyes snapped open. Marlie's face had gone white. She clapped her palm over her mouth and ran from the room. Seconds later the unmistakable sound of retching drifted through Chasing Rainbows. He'd never had that effect on a woman before.

"Wha'd ya do? Kiss her again?"

Jake stood in the doorway, glaring at Colin as if he'd witnessed the entire incident. Maybe he had. It wasn't as though Colin had been thinking of anything but her. Not only had he forgotten his vow not to touch her, he'd forgotten they were in a small house with ten sleeping children.

Boy, would he make a lousy father. Something Colin had never doubted.

"Women don't usually throw up when I kiss them, kid."

"I'd throw up if someone kissed me." Jake tilted his head as if listening to another voice. "Ned says he'd definitely throw up if you kissed him."

Colin fought not to laugh. He kinda liked Jake. Too bad Jake didn't like him. Or Ned, either.

A pained moan trickled down the hall from the bathroom. "I'd better check on your teacher."

"If she's barfin' 'cause of you, maybe *I'd* better check on her."

Colin hesitated. Though he doubted his touch had made Marlie sick, he also doubted she'd want him to see her with her head in the toilet. Women were funny that way.

"Maybe you'd better," he agreed.

Jake hurried off. Colin waited in the hall, staring at the sleeping children, terrified they'd all wake up and come after him.

"Miss Marlie, you okay?"

Colin glanced in Jake's direction. The little boy pressed his ear to the bathroom door, nodded, then trotted back to Colin.

"She's sick."

"Gee, thanks. I didn't know."

Jake's face scrunched into a confused scowl. He was obviously too young for sarcasm.

"Never mind," Colin said. "Does she need help?"

"I think she can spew all by herself."

Jake disappeared into the office, and Colin went back to staring at the sleeping children. It seemed like forever, but at last the bathroom door opened and Marlie appeared. She was still pale. Her hand shook when she swiped it over her face, and she zigzagged when she walked as if she was dizzy. She'd stuffed her glasses in the pocket of her shirt, and she blinked owlishly as she swayed.

Alarmed, Colin hurried toward her. "What's the matter?"

"Must have been something I ate."

"We ate the same things."

"Except for the —" Marlie swallowed, slapped her palm over mouth and ran back into the bathroom, slamming the door.

"Tuna sandwich," Colin finished. "Hell."

He'd been in enough foreign countries to learn that food poisoning was a tricky illness. Certain types took weeks to materialize, making it impossible to know where

128

you got it in the first place. Other kinds sent a sufferer to their knees within the hour. Only one thing was the same in every case — the victim wished he was dead.

Someone tugged on his pant leg. Colin glanced down to discover Katrina, the meanest little girl in Wind Lake, rubbing sleepy eyes.

"Gotta go," she mumbled.

"School's not out for a few hours."

"No! Gotta *go! Now.*"

Oh. That kind of *go.* Colin practically ran down the hall. He tapped on the door. A groan was his answer.

"Uh, Marlie. There's a little girl who has to, um, you know?"

The toilet flushed. Water ran. The door opened. Marlie stepped out and Katrina ran in.

"I know," Marlie whispered, her voice scratchy and weak.

"You'd better go home."

She laughed, though no sound came out, then she leaned her head against the wall and took several deep breaths.

"I'm okay," she murmured as if to herself. "I'm okay."

"You're not. Go home and lie down."

"And what about the kids?"

"They can go home, too."

"Do you live in La-La Land or only visit there twice a year?"

"What?"

"There's no one at home or these kids wouldn't be here. Their parents work."

"All of them?"

"Yes. It might say preschool, but if you knew anything about preschools, you'd know they're open for two or three hours. Chasing Rainbows is also a day care. I can't just close up and lie down."

She clapped her hand over her mouth, glanced at the still-closed bathroom door and raced into the office. Colin was just in time to see her stick her head into the garbage can. Jake, who had his head under the desk, was lucky enough to miss it.

"Don't you have a substitute or something? You can't be here every single day. You have to get sick sometime."

Marlie set down the garbage and washed her face with a damp paper towel. "There *is* someone who fills in when I'm sick. Carol. But she's gone."

"Gone?"

"On vacation. Who gets sick in August?" Marlie snorted. "Apparently me."

"What about your mom?"

"What about her?"

"Can't she come over?"

"You *are* delusional. My mom doesn't know what year it is. She can't be responsible for ten kids under the age of five."

"Right now, neither can you."

"I'll manage. Tiffany will be here at three."

"Get Tiffany over here now."

"Tiffany is seventeen. She can't leave school any more than I can."

She crept to her desk and laid her head on the top. Jake crawled out from under it, took one glance at her and disappeared. The guinea pig was still on the loose, but Colin had bigger troubles at the moment than a renegade rat-thing.

"Go home," he repeated.

"Can't." The word was muffled, as if her lips were pressed into the desktop. She no doubt felt like warmed-over death right now — a phrase of his mother's and incredibly apt when applied to food poisoning.

"I'll stay."

She looked up so fast her eyes crossed. He winced, then handed her the garbage can. She shook her head, did some wincing of her own, then set her cheek back against the desk.

"No. You're not certified."

He glanced at his watch. "It's an hour,

131

Marlie. I can handle ten kids for an hour. You can't."

"I'm okay."

"You aren't, and it's going to get worse."

"How do you know?"

"Because I've been there. Pretty soon you're going to live in that bathroom. If I were you, I'd get home before the next symptom hits."

She lifted her head, more slowly this time, and stared at him with a question in her eyes. He nodded. There was no reason to put into words what the next symptom would be. Stomach ailments were of two kinds — and food poisoning made use of both of them.

As if to illustrate his point, Marlie's belly rumbled so loudly the sound seemed to fill the room. Her eyes flew wide and she stood, then headed for the door at a brisk walk, throwing final instructions over her shoulder.

"Call me if you have any questions."

"We'll be fine," he returned, but she was already out the back door.

He hurried over and glanced out the window. She was losing what was left of her lunch behind the geraniums.

Colin turned and contemplated the nine lumps on the floor. Katrina must have

132

slipped back in and gone to sleep. Lucky him.

One of the girls shifted and sighed, "Mommy" in her sleep. Colin held his breath until she settled again.

Making his way back to the office, he had a great idea. If he was quiet, maybe they'd sleep until Tiffany came.

Slowly, gently, he closed the office door. Then sat in Marlie's chair and leaned back with a smile. It was worth a try.

Unfortunately, he'd forgotten one thing.

"Gotcha," Jake announced, and deposited Houdini on Colin's head.

CHAPTER EIGHT

Colin let out a howl to rival that of any animal inhabiting the forest around Wind Lake. The rat-thing jumped on to his lap, scrambled down his leg and piddled on his foot.

Jake started giggling, then couldn't stop. He laughed until he fell on the floor. He rolled around on the carpet the entire time Colin wiped guinea pig pee off his leather shoes. He laughed so long Colin worried he might have to clean up after Jake, too.

The door opened. Colin's dream of presenting Tiffany with a roomful of sleeping children evaporated as nine pairs of curious eyes met his.

"Wha'd ya do to Jake?"

Colin recognized the speaker as Victor, the defeated bathroom-line bandit from yesterday.

"I didn't do anything to him. Maybe you should ask what he did to me."

Victor shrugged. "Wha'd he do?"

Colin opened his mouth, but Jake sat up, stopped laughing and pointed at him. "Didja hear him scream?"

The children nodded.

"Like a girl."

Colin snapped his mouth shut and frowned. Someone giggled in the back, then in the front, then on the side. Pretty soon they were all laughing so hard he feared a flood.

"All right, all right. Get in line for the bathroom."

Chaos erupted. He should have let them laugh.

Within minutes, there were three fistfights, two wrestling matches, three shrieking girls and two crying boys. Jake was still laughing.

"Enough!" Colin roared.

Everyone went silent, but only for a moment. The hitching sound was his first clue. Seconds later everyone was crying.

Colin stared at the mess he'd made. He didn't know what to do.

Jake yanked on his pants. Colin flinched, expecting the boy to shove Houdini up the cuff. Instead, Jake crooked his finger.

Colin lowered to Jake's level. "Never yell. 'Specially at girls. They cry over nothin'."

"Thanks for the tip," Colin muttered, and glanced at his watch.

Holy hell, he'd only been alone with

135

them for ten minutes.

Things went downhill from there.

One little girl needed help getting dressed after her turn in the bathroom. Since he couldn't help her, he sent in a few others. They had a water fight.

Alerted by the shrieking and the laughter, Colin rapped on the door, warned them he was coming, then promptly skated across the wet tile on the heels of his best shoes. He landed on his tailbone in a puddle. When he tried to get to his feet, he ended up planting the knees of his slacks in two inches of water. Everyone thought that was great entertainment.

He used a roll of paper towels to sop up the flood. By the time he returned to the main room, three children had begun to fingerpaint the carpet, two were swinging by the curtains. The front door was open, and when he counted heads, he came up with eight.

"Son of a —"

"Goat!" one of the children shouted.

Goat? Well, he didn't have time to get to the bottom of that right now, as much as he might like to.

Colin stepped outside. He could hear the missing children, but he couldn't see them — until he raised his gaze. Two little girls were hanging upside down from a tree limb ten feet off the ground.

His heart nearly stopped. He ran across the lawn. The girls giggled and waved.

"Come down here." He reached up to catch them.

They swung just out of his reach and began to make monkey noises. Colin glanced at his watch and nearly passed out. Thirty minutes until Tiffany.

He managed to coax the girls from the tree with a banana he found in the office. By then the other children were outside, and several passing cars had stopped to watch the show. Marlie was going to kill him. If he didn't kill himself first.

Since the kids were eyeing the banana as if it were the last food on the face of the earth, Colin had an idea.

"Snacks for everyone inside." He brushed his hands together. "Like taking candy from a baby."

Colin wasn't feeling so smug an hour later. He was still alone, no sign of Tiffany, and all the food was gone. The children stared at him expectantly.

"Now what?" he asked.

They all started talking at once. He'd

discovered that if he raised a hand and ignored everything they said, eventually they stopped talking. He was losing circulation in his arm, but his headache had backed off.

"Jake? What do you guys usually do after your nap and your snack?"

"We play games with Tiffany until our parents come for us." He frowned. "Hey, where is Tiffany?"

The glance Jake gave him told Colin the boy thought he'd done something with her. He'd like to wring her neck.

"What kind of games?" he asked warily.

There was no way he was playing hide-and-seek with these kids. He'd never find them.

"The Matching Game. Chutes and Ladders. Candyland."

Victor sidled up to him. "Don't play Candyland with Katrina. If she doesn't get Queen Frostine, she kicks you." Victor rubbed his ankle and grimaced.

After hearing that little tidbit, Colin was afraid, if he let them play games, they'd be rolling around on the floor fighting within minutes. "Uh, do you ever just watch TV?"

"Nope. Miss Marlie said this is school. We can rot our minds any old time. She don't even have a TV here." Victor rolled his eyes as if the lack of a television was the biggest disappointment in his short life.

Colin let his gaze wander around the room. The place didn't look good. He could imagine what the parents would think if they saw the trash, the paint, the overturned chairs and dumped bookcase.

"Let's have a race," he began.

"What kind of race?"

"Half of us start on this side of the room, and half on that side. Whoever has their side of the room clean first wins."

"Wins what?"

Colin narrowed his eyes at Jake, but the boy just stared back innocently. "Whatever happened to winning for the sake of winning?"

"What's that?" Jake asked. All the other children shrugged.

"What do you want?"

"Dollar."

"A dollar?"

"For everyone on the winnin' team."

"Haven't you ever heard of a quarter?"

Jake wrinkled his nose in disgust. "Even the fairy gives a dollar."

Fairy? For a minute Colin wondered if there was actually a person of the gay persuasion living in Wind Lake. He couldn't imagine it. Then he realized Jake was talking about the tooth fairy.

"A dollar a tooth?"

"Yeah."

Times sure had changed. He'd gotten a dime for every tooth, a quarter only if his mom didn't have correct change. But then, with six kids in the family, that was a whole helluva lot of teeth to buy.

During the time he'd spent thinking and arguing with Jake, some of the kids had drifted toward the paint again. Panic made him blurt, "Fine. I'll give a dollar to each of the winners, okay?"

They scattered.

If Colin had needed any more proof of the mercenary society being created through the nation's children, he'd have had it right here.

"Kids today," he muttered, then laughed at himself. He sounded just like his dad. When had that happened?

He went into the office and tried to find a phone number for Tiffany. No such luck.

He considered calling Marlie, but discarded the idea. He was doing all right. The kids were fine. He could handle things until five o'clock. Piece of cake.

Colin sat in Marlie's chair, put his feet on the desk and leaned back.

The fire alarm went off.

He swung his feet to the floor, stepped on Houdini, flinched at the animal's screech. But the guinea pig was uninjured, as evidenced by the speed with which he disappeared from the room. Colin was right on his heels.

The kids were shrieking. His heart was pounding so loudly he feared it would burst from his chest.

"Stop, drop and roll," he muttered. "Stop, drop and roll."

The sight that greeted him halted Colin in his tracks. No one was on fire, thank God. Instead, the children danced in the water that poured from the sprinklers installed in the ceiling.

Smoke rose in a gray, dying plume from a heap of smoldering garbage in the center of the room. Colin strode over and kicked the pile apart, stomping on the cinders.

By the time he was done, he was as soaked as the children, but not half as happy about it.

"Who did this?" he demanded, pointing at the pile.

A little boy he hadn't met yet raised his hand. "My daddy always burns the garbage in the yard."

"Does this look like a yard to you?"

"You said we couldn't go outside."

Colin's headache was back, and it was worse than ever.

"Did anyone ever tell you not to play with matches?"

"Sure." The kid dug in his pocket, pulled out a lighter, flicked the flame to life. "This isn't a match."

Colin swiped the thing from the kid's hand. "It's still fire. Where did you get this?"

"Found it on the street. Fire's my favorite thing."

Alarmed, Colin put the lighter into his own pocket. The kid was a pyro at age four. What was the world coming to? Sadly, he had a pretty good idea. The world was coming to an end and soon.

"What's your name, kid?"

The boy zipped his lip, but the rest of the children answered in a singsong voice, "Looo-is."

"Louis?"

The kid nodded. No wonder he liked to set fire to things. Colin would, too, if his parents had named him Louis. What were people thinking? Whatever happened to good solid names like John, James, Matthew? He was sounding more and more like his father with every passing moment.

Water dripped down each face, including

his own. "Change your clothes. Take turns. Then we'll go outside."

"Hey, cappin's brother?"

Colin glanced at Jake, who was grinning at him from his post by the window.

"Yeah?"

"There's firemen comin' up the walk. Should I let 'em in?"

Marlie had never felt so awful in her life. She was living in the bathroom. Every time she tried to lie down, she had to rush back. She might as well put her bed in here.

Her mother checked on her at each commercial. She'd brought ginger ale, which tasted good on the way down. Not so good on the way back up.

Marlie lost track of time. She'd fallen into a doze with her head resting on the toilet seat when a demented pounding at the door made her gasp and jerk completely awake.

"Peanut, you okay?"

Garth.

Marlie groaned. "Go 'way. I'm dying."

"Can I come in?"

"Never."

"Your mom called. She's worried."

She'd called a cook and not the doctor? Marlie wasn't surprised.

"I ate something that didn't agree with me."

"You've been in there for two hours, according to your mother. I'd say you ate something that gave you food poisoning."

That much she knew.

"Go away."

"If you don't come out of there in sixty seconds, I'm breaking down the door. You know I can do it."

He could. And would. Marlie dragged herself to her feet, brushed her teeth, splashed water on her face and opened the door. Without her glasses, which she'd left on her dresser, since she'd rather not see what she was throwing up, Garth's face was blurry. She could still see his frown.

"You look like hell."

She slammed the door in his face. Before she could flick the lock and go back to her favorite toilet, he opened it again. Garth might be big, but that didn't mean he wasn't quick.

He took her hand and drew her into the hall.

"Come on, Peanut. Time to get in bed. I made you some tea."

"I'll just throw it up."

"Better that you have something to throw up than nothing."

Marlie was too tired to argue. She let Garth lead her into the bedroom and gently shove her onto the bed. He removed her shoes.

"I'll be right back."

While he was gone, she lost her clothes and found her flannel pajamas. She'd started to shiver with reaction.

Garth returned with the tea, and he was right — she did feel better sipping it beneath the covers. He sat on the bed. The mattress rocked like a small boat under his weight, and Marlie nearly spilled tea down her chin.

"Should I call the doctor?" he asked.

"No. I'm better already." She tried to smile, but from Garth's alarmed expression, she hadn't managed more than a grimace. Marlie hid the lower half of her face behind the mug of tea.

"You need to stay hydrated. Don't try to eat until you can keep liquids down for several hours."

"Thank you, Dr. Lundquist. Where did you learn so much about food poisoning?"

Sadness flickered through his eyes. "Nika had it once."

Marlie sighed. No matter how hard she tried to avoid any mention of Nika, sometimes she inadvertently brought her up.

"Besides —" Garth tried to laugh, but he couldn't manage one any better than she'd managed a smile "— the treatment for food poisoning is handy for a chef to know."

"No one would ever get food poisoning in your place!"

He patted her hand. "Thanks. I do my best, but who knows if my suppliers are as conscientious? Accidents happen. Statistically, the chances of getting some kind of food poisoning in your lifetime are pretty high. Higher if you eat in restaurants a lot. Astronomical if you travel out of the country."

"Remind me never to travel out of the country."

As if she ever would.

"I'm an encyclopedia of food-related information. Maybe I should challenge your mom to some high-stakes *Jeopardy!*"

"She'd kill you."

"I know."

Marlie had sipped half the tea and her stomach felt full. Perhaps she should package botulism as the new diet of the stars.

Garth took the mug and set it on her nightstand. Then he pressed his palm to her forehead and frowned. "You're hot."

"I'm freezing."

"Fever. Your skin's on fire, so the air feels chilly. I'd give you aspirin, but not on an empty stomach. Want a cold cloth?"

Marlie winced at the idea of a cold cloth. Her back hurt from shivering.

"Not right now. I think I'll just sleep. Maybe when I wake up, this will all be a dream."

"Don't count on it. You should probably stay home tomorrow."

She snorted. "Too bad I can't. Carol is on vacation, remember?"

He blinked. "Then who's with the kids?"

"Tiffany, by now." Marlie looked away. "Colin stayed with them."

"That pretty boy?" Garth jumped up as if he meant to run across the street and rescue his son from an ogre. "Are you nuts?"

Marlie grabbed his hand. "Relax. I'm sure he handled things just fine for an hour."

Garth rolled his eyes. Marlie's chest went tight with guilt. Maybe she shouldn't have left Colin with the kids.

"I didn't know what else to do," she murmured.

"You could have called me."

"And made you close up for the afternoon? You can't afford that."

He shrugged, but she knew it was true. In a small town like Wind Lake, going out to eat, even at the café, was a luxury. Garth earned just enough to keep him and Jake in food and clothing. Living above the restaurant was the only place they could manage.

"One day wouldn't hurt me."

"It would hurt *me*. Everything's fine," she assured him, as well as herself. "I'll be back at work tomorrow."

Marlie leaned her head against the pillow and closed her eyes. She still felt awful. But as long as she was able to walk, she'd be at work. She couldn't count the number of times she'd gone in when she wasn't up to snuff.

Until they built up an immunity to the various germs floating around, teachers got sick. Usually the first year was a maze of minor colds and the flu. After that, it was easier. Truthfully, Marlie hadn't been ill in a long time. Of course, she hadn't gotten ill this time from the germs of a child but from a tuna sandwich.

"When's he leaving?"

She'd been drifting toward sleep, expecting Garth to slip out and pick up Jake, when his question made her start.

"What? Who?"

"Luchetti. I don't like him staying here."

Garth's comment reminded her of his behavior last night. She'd meant to talk to him when he came to get Jake. Now would have to do.

Marlie sat up and shook off the lethargy as best she could. "What's the matter with you, Garth? Colin's searching for Bobby, and you're treating him like a serial killer."

"Bobby's not here, so why is he?"

"Colin thinks he may show up."

"So what if he does? You can always call the family. It's the miracle of modern telephones. Doesn't Luchetti have somewhere else he can wait?"

Marlie blinked. She had no idea where Colin lived.

Quickly she explained Colin's reason for being here.

"That doesn't make any sense," Garth muttered. "Why would your captain write a note like that? Why would he send his brother to Wind Lake?"

"Your guess is as good as ours. But you can understand why he can't leave."

Suspicion clouded Garth's eyes. "Did you see the letter? Was it Bobby's handwriting?"

"Yes. Wait a minute — what are you suggesting?"

"Anyone can make up anything and you'd believe them, Marlie. You're much too trusting."

"You think Colin forged the letter? What possible reason could he have for doing such a thing?"

"I don't know. Just seems strange that a guy like him would hang around a town like this for any reason. I'm sure he's got better places to be, more interesting people to see."

Though Marlie had thought the same thing, she wasn't going to let Garth know it. She also wasn't going to let him know how much his comment hurt. She knew she wasn't interesting, but she didn't expect her best friend to think so.

"You liked Colin well enough yesterday when he was in the café. What changed?"

"He moved in on you."

"Moved in on me? What happened to he should snatch me up before his brother does?"

"I didn't mean the first day."

"What difference does it make?"

"Marlie. Peanut." He sighed and spread his hands. "Men are . . . pigs."

A startled bubble of laughter tickled her

throat. Since Garth didn't appear as if he was going to laugh anytime soon, she forced it back down with a cough.

"How do you figure?" she managed.

"They're only after one thing."

She couldn't resist. "What thing?"

He cut her a quick glance, saw the amusement on her face and cursed. "This isn't funny. Guys like him have a girl in every port."

"He isn't in the navy."

"He may as well be. He's going to get in your pants, then leave you behind."

Her amusement faded as she started to get mad. "Well, isn't that flattering."

"Listen to me. He comes from a different world. One where he can kiss a girl the first day he meets her and no one thinks any less of him — or her. But that's not our world."

"You think less of me because I kissed him?"

"Of course not."

Marlie closed her eyes. She just wanted to sleep.

"You don't have to worry." She glanced at Garth with a wan smile. "He apologized for kissing me. It was probably just a knee-jerk reaction to any female in the vicinity."

"I still don't trust him."

"Relax. If there's one thing I'm sure of, it's that Colin Luchetti is trustworthy."

Garth sighed and walked to the window. He twitched aside the curtain, then stiffened and pressed his face to the glass.

"What's the matter?"

"Mr. Trustworthy appears to have set your preschool on fire."

"What?"

Marlie swung her feet out of bed, tried to stand and almost fell on her face. Garth caught her and led her to the window.

He was right. Even though her vision was blurry, the entire Wind Lake Fire Department appeared to be parked in front of Chasing Rainbows. Marlie's stomach lurched.

The children. Her business. Colin.

She began to run, but the combination of adrenaline and exertion made her detour into the bathroom where she lost the tea.

As she lay there weakly retching, Garth hurried out the front door. She couldn't blame him. She'd have done the same thing.

If she could walk.

CHAPTER NINE

Colin had talked his way out of a lot of things. Prison in Pakistan, a firing squad in Iraq, detention in the seventh grade, being grounded by his mother. But talking the Wind Lake Fire Department out of closing down Chasing Rainbows was one of the toughest things he'd ever done.

Still, he managed. By agreeing to have the place professionally cleaned and cleared by tomorrow.

He didn't care what he had to do, who he had to pay or how much. The thought of Marlie's face when she saw what he'd allowed to happen was bad enough. He couldn't tell her that she was closed for business.

Setting the children to the task of stuffing soggy trash into garbage bags, Colin got out the phone book and prepared to beg. The door opened and shut before he made the first call.

He glanced up from the tiny schoolroom desk he'd scrunched himself into — he wasn't leaving these heathens alone ever again — and was shocked to see Garth and not Marlie. Maybe she was sicker than he thought.

He picked up the phone, but he didn't know her number. So he stood and headed for the door.

"I'm glad you're here," he said to Garth. "I have to check on Marlie."

The big man grabbed his arm. Colin had been grabbed by bigger, meaner, nastier men than Lundquist. He twisted out of Garth's grasp and kept on walking.

However, Garth slammed the door as soon as Colin opened it and kept his huge hand in the way.

"Move it or lose it. I have to see if she's okay."

"She's fine. What in —" Garth broke off with a wary glance at the children. "What happened?"

"If she's fine, why isn't she here?"

"Because she's unable to leave the bathroom right now, even though she wanted to."

Colin cursed. All the children gasped.

"Nice one," Garth muttered. "They'll be repeating that for a week."

"Sorry. I'm not used to kids."

"Really? Could have fooled me."

Colin frowned at Garth's sarcasm. "I did my best."

"I guess your best wasn't good enough."

Garth grabbed Colin's arm again and shoved him toward the office. Since Colin agreed they needed to do this in private, he went. Once there, they stood just inside the room watching the children.

"How did you manage to set the place on fire?" Garth asked.

"Wasn't me."

Garth made an exasperated sound. "Where's Tiffany? Did she run screaming at the first sign of trouble?"

"She was never here in the first place."

"You mean you've been alone with them the entire afternoon?" Garth's voice and face reflected his horror.

"My thoughts exactly."

Garth sighed and rubbed his forehead. "Just tell me what happened."

Colin did.

"Didn't anyone ever mention you shouldn't turn your back on them?"

Now that Garth brought it up, Marlie had. Colin had just forgotten in all the excitement.

"You may as well go home," Garth continued. "I'll take it from here."

"I'll let you. But I'm going to make a few calls before I head back to the Andersons'."

Garth narrowed his eyes. "I meant, go back wherever it is you came from."

Colin, who had been headed toward Marlie's desk, paused and turned around. "What do you have against me?"

"Marlie and I have been friends since we were five."

"Congratulations."

"I don't think you're good for her."

"I'm not here for her."

"You just keep tellin' everyone that. Maybe someone will believe you. But don't count on it being me."

Suddenly Colin understood Garth's hostility. "You want her," he blurted.

Garth blinked. His shock was obvious. "We're friends."

"Right. Men and women are friends *all* the time."

"Get your mind out of the gutter."

"You went there first."

Colin might as well stick his thumbs in his ears, wave his fingers at the man and shout, "Na-na-na-nana!"

Garth crossed the short distance between them, stopping only an inch away. Towering over Colin, he murmured, "Don't screw with me, Luchetti. You won't like what happens."

Colin had never taken well to intimidation. Maybe that came from being the third child in a family of six. His older brothers had shoved him around, the younger ones always tried to. He'd spent most of his youth shoving back.

"Don't threaten me."

"Consider it a promise, then. Make her cry, and I'll make you beg — to die."

Colin would have laughed at that dialogue, straight out of a James Bond movie yet to come, except Garth was serious.

Well, he didn't plan on making Marlie cry. He didn't plan on making Marlie anything, including his next girlfriend, lover or wife. So there wasn't going to be any problem.

However, he decided not to tell Garth that. Let him figure it out for himself.

By the time Marlie managed to get out of the bathroom, the fire engines were gone. All appeared peaceful across the street as parents arrived to pick up their children.

Her mother was watching *Jeopardy!* Between the first and second round, she informed Marlie, "Garth called. Everything's fine. He'll take care of closing up, and Colin will be home later."

Fine told her nothing. *Fine* could mean

anything from a false alarm to a blaze the size of an elephant — as long as the children were safe.

She considered going across the street, but she felt so weak she didn't know if she'd make it. She could see the headline in the *Weekly* already: Preschool teacher collapses on the lawn of her own preschool. Picture on page twelve.

Better to let Garth handle things.

Marlie went back to bed. She awoke when the front door closed. Putting on her glasses, she glanced at the clock. She'd slept through the dinner hour. She felt better — almost normal, even a bit hungry.

The low murmur of Colin's voice from the front room made her sit up. He was just getting back now?

She climbed out of bed and went searching for a robe, but before she could find it, a soft knock came on her door. She dived under the covers.

"Yes?"

Colin stuck his head into the room. He smiled and her stomach danced. Luckily there was nothing left in it to lose, although that hadn't stopped it before.

"Can I come in?"

She hesitated, unnerved at having him in her room when she wore only her pajamas.

She didn't even want to think about how awful she looked.

When had that started to matter? Must have been yesterday.

She hadn't cared when Garth tromped into her bedroom, hadn't minded when he sat right on her bed, but Colin was different.

She pulled the covers up to her chin so he wouldn't see her breasts straining against the buttons of her top, then nodded for him to come inside.

"I suppose you heard what happened." He pulled the chair from her desk nearer to the bed.

"Not really."

His eyes widened. "I figured your watchdog would have called you immediately."

"My watchdog?"

"Garth. He's very protective."

Marlie groaned. "What did he do?"

Colin contemplated her for a long, silent moment, then shrugged. "Nothing. He helped with the kids, but . . ."

Uneasy, she straightened and the covers slithered to her waist. Colin's gaze slid from her face to her chest and stuck there.

She glanced down, afraid the buttons had burst open, unable to contain her chest any longer. Instead, the spikes of her nipples thrust against the thin, soft material of her shirt.

His eyes lifted. In them was an expression she could not define. One that made her cheeks heat. Slowly she covered herself again.

He licked his lips, cleared his throat, glanced away. Marlie wanted to apologize, but she wasn't sure how or even what she'd be apologizing for.

Instead, she forced herself to ask the question she'd been saving since the firefighters arrived. "What happened?"

His eyes flicked toward her, then down to his shoes. There was a streak across one tip, as if he'd drizzled ammonia on the leather. She had a pretty good idea what had happened.

Houdini strikes again. Marlie's lips twitched, but her amusement was short-lived.

"There was a little misunderstanding about what to do with the trash."

"How little?"

"I took care of everything. That's why I'm so late. I had to make some calls, wait for them to show up, get them started."

He spoke quickly as if to allay her fears. But since he'd told her nothing, he only succeeded in frightening her more.

"Call who? To start what?"

"Um. Well, uh . . ." He glanced away again.

"What did you do?"

Visions flickered, a gutted day care, the books turned to ashes, furniture charred and black, everything gray and soggy, as steam rose from the damp ruins.

Chasing Rainbows — her baby — dead and gone.

Dizziness came over Marlie in a nauseating wave. Her skin went hot, her head swam. She clapped her hand over her mouth.

Colin jumped up so fast, his chair fell over. He grabbed the supersize mixing bowl she'd stolen from the kitchen for just this emergency and shoved it into her lap. Then he patted her on the back — too hard — as if trying to dislodge something in her throat. If he kept that up, he'd dislodge a lung.

"I'm okay," she managed, her voice hitching with the force of his pats.

She pushed the bowl into his hands in an attempt to get him to stop comforting her. He had no choice but to take the thing. Then he stood there staring into its empty depths as he shuffled his feet. After a few moments, he set the bowl back on her nightstand.

"There was just a little fire," he murmured.

"How little?"

Circling his arms, he lifted his brows. "About so big. The real problem was the sprinklers. You'll be happy to know they work."

She groaned and fell back on the bed, put her palm to her forehead. She couldn't tell if she had a fever, since her hand was as hot as the rest of her.

"Can I get you anything?"

Now that she was no longer shivering, a cold compress just might help. "There's a washcloth on the sink in the bathroom. Can you wet it and bring it here?"

"Sure." He practically ran into the half bath that connected to her bedroom.

Marlie had a panicked moment where she wondered if she'd left anything embarrassing lying about in there. Then she remembered that she had no life, and therefore owned nothing embarrassing.

Colin returned quickly and plopped the cloth onto her forehead. The dizziness intensified. He'd used warm water.

She yanked it off before her internal temperature skyrocketed as high as the moon.

"Something wrong?"

His face anxious, she didn't have the heart to tell him the heat of the cloth made her head ache. Instead, she quickly wiped her face and laid the thing aside.

"Thank you."

He smiled and sat down. "Can I get you anything else? You must be hungry. I'll go buy a pizza."

Her stomach lurched.

He interpreted her expression of horror as lack of enthusiasm for pizza. "Tacos? Fried chicken? I know — a cheeseburger."

"Stop." Marlie clapped one hand over her mouth and held the other up, palm in his direction.

A few moments later, she felt confident enough to lower her arms. "You've never had to take care of anyone who was sick, have you?"

His expression turned sheepish. "That obvious?"

"Yeah."

"Sorry. I'm better with first aid. Scrapes, sprains, bullet holes — I'm your man."

"Bullet holes!" she squeaked.

"I'm only kidding."

But she had to wonder. "Let's get back to the fire."

"Do we have to?"

"Yes," she said in her sternest teacher voice.

He told her what happened. She wasn't sure if she should laugh or cry. In the end she did neither.

"I'll have to close tomorrow."

"No. It'll be fixed by then."

She snorted. "I'll be lucky if it's fixed by Halloween."

"I called a fire-cleanup company. Told them to be done by tomorrow or don't bother to come."

"And that worked?"

"With the added incentive of a big, fat check."

Marlie gulped. "I can't afford that."

"I can."

"Oh, no. I won't let you —"

"Too late. I already did. The fire was my fault."

"No. I never should have left."

"I should be able to handle ten kids."

"Why? Should I be able to handle —" her mind groped for an example "— corresponding foreignly?"

He laughed. "There's a big difference between my job and yours."

She stiffened. "Oh, and what's that?"

"Yours is a helluva lot harder."

He had to get out of her room. If he kept hanging out here, he might just end up there — in her bed, in her.

"I'll let you rest," he blurted. "Good night."

Her softly murmured " 'Night" trilled along his skin like a whisper.

"Let's play *Name That Tune*," Julie called as he ran past.

He didn't answer as he took the stairs two at a time.

Safe in his room, he leaned his hot forehead against the cool, solid wood of the door. He was depraved. How could he lust after a woman who was sick in bed?

But Marlie hadn't looked sick. She'd looked soft, warm, sexy and inviting, and she'd smelled like . . . vanilla. He was definitely depraved if the scent of vanilla made him picture an orgy just for two.

Trying to drown images of Marlie in bed all alone, he checked his e-mail. Nothing from Bobby, three from his mother, one from Dean and two from FARMERSWIFE, which had to be Kim. He downloaded them all without reading them, then moved to the window.

If he turned his head just so, he could see the day care. Now he knew that

Marlie's bedroom was right beneath his own. Even though it was located near the back of the house and on the side, she'd seen the fire trucks, the gawkers. He could imagine what she'd thought.

Yet she hadn't yelled, she hadn't thrown anything, she hadn't ordered him out of her house, out of her life. What kind of woman was she?

His mother and his sister both would have let him have it, then forgiven him. Women he'd dated would have given him the silent treatment, refusing to speak to him until he'd groveled a while.

Even when he'd botched his attempt to nurse and comfort, Marlie had merely smiled and teased him a little. He wasn't certain what to make of her.

He wasn't certain what to make of himself, either. He'd never been one to be overcome with feelings for a woman. He liked them well enough. Women were pretty, they smelled good, felt even better — but he'd never cared what a woman thought of him or worried about what she might say.

Marlie was different. He liked her. He wanted to be with her. When he was with her, he wanted to touch her. When he touched her, he wanted to kiss her.

Colin cursed. He couldn't. He *had* to remember that.

But when her bedclothes had pooled around her waist and her eyes had gone wide behind those great big glasses, then her nipples had gone hard, his mind had gone . . . into the gutter. Garth hadn't been far wrong.

In his imagination, he'd joined her on the bed, removed her glasses gently before pressing his mouth to the ivory hollow of her throat. He'd let his fingers loosen the buttons of her pajamas, felt her breasts spill into his hands. The scent of her skin, the slide of her hair . . .

He'd had to force away the fantasy before he disgraced himself. His slacks were silk. They didn't disguise an erection all that well. Before today, they hadn't had to.

What was it about sweet, innocent Marlie that made him want to rip off her clothes and discover if she was as enticing as she smelled?

"Brother's girl. Brother's girl." He thumped himself on the head. "She's Bobby's until further notice."

In an attempt to keep his thoughts off Marlie, Colin turned to the waiting e-mails. His mother's were succinct.

167

Turn on your phone!
Today, please.
Now!

Even though he'd sworn not to, he *had* shut off his cell phone while he was taking care of the children. He couldn't attend to both. Hell, he couldn't attend to one at a time.

Shaking his head in disgust at his ineptitude, Colin powered up the phone. The thing immediately started beeping with messages.

After ascertaining that none of them were from Bobby, he tossed the phone onto the bed and continued with the e-mail, reading Dean's first.

Hey, loser. Better get your act together. If you don't watch it, Mom will come up there. And you DON'T want that. Take my word for it. She's still one step away from ignition most days.

I told her you'd call if there was news. But we're all getting kind of worried. This isn't like Bobby.

Hell. Gotta go. A doodle just went on the bed. Mom is going to have a stroke.

You don't know anyone who wants a dog — or five — do you?

Colin smiled. Reading his brother's letter, he could almost hear Dean talking. Sometimes he missed his family, but mostly he didn't.

Sure, he loved them, but after eighteen years of being crowded into one house — no privacy, no quiet time, no room of his own — he preferred loving them from a distance.

Colin opened Kim's first e-mail, which appeared to be gibberish. He frowned, hoping she hadn't sent him a virus. He clicked on the second e-mail. This one made more sense.

Sorry. Zsa Zsa appears to be some sort of genius. I've already had to put the phone on top of the refrigerator. She mastered speed dial at nine months.

I took five seconds to go to the bathroom — and I can go in five seconds, too, a toddler does amazing things for speed in daily living — and came back to discover she sent a note to my entire address book. I only hope *zxkldy5yurtjnv99yrlrtjk* doesn't mean anything in secret code. :) I can't lift the computer any higher than it already is.

It sure would be nice if you came home and met your niece before she turns thirty. I think you two would get along great. She's an adventurer like you.

Is Bobby okay? I know you didn't tell Mom anything because she'd freak. And Dad would start smoking again — which would also make Mom freak. You know how they are. But you can tell me. Right?

"Wrong," Colin muttered.

Even if there'd been anything to tell, he didn't have the balls to go behind his mom's back and tell Kim. He wouldn't live to see another sunrise.

His mother and his sister had fought their way through Kim's youth. Only when she returned after an absence of eight years, and revealed all the secrets that had made her run in the first place, had the two found common ground. Now they were pals. But that didn't mean he was going to get in between them. He wasn't a complete idiot.

Colin quickly typed a note to Kim and Dean reiterating that he knew nothing. After checking his phone messages — three more from his mother and one from a carpet-cleaning company offering to clean his nonexistent carpet — he answered his mother's e-mail.

"Nothing new," he wrote. "Don't call us, we'll call you." That was sure to piss Eleanor off, but right now he was too tired to care.

He managed to shut down his computer, change out of another pair of ruined slacks — one more day and he'd be out of pants — then brush his teeth before exhaustion claimed him. Maybe it was the fresh air, or the stress, but he couldn't keep his eyes open past nine o'clock. Some suave, sophisticated world traveler he was.

He awoke to the sound of his name being repeated in a child's whisper, which appeared to be one level below a shout. Something was on his chest, something heavy that made it hard to breathe. For a minute he wondered if he'd been in an accident and broken his ribs.

Colin opened his eyes and gave a mighty start. Jake's nose nearly touched his.

"You're awake." The boy sat up and bounced, landing on Colin's stomach without warning.

"I am now," he choked out.

"Good. 'Cause Miss Marlie said I shouldn't wake you."

"Was there something you wanted, Jake?"

171

"Nope. Me and Ned just wanted to see ya."

The boy swung his legs over Colin's chest and landed with both feet on the floor. Colin narrowed his eyes. The kid was up to something. Yesterday Colin had been very low on Jake's list of favorite people, and suddenly Jake wanted to see him?

"I don't think so," Colin muttered.

"Huh?" Jake had been creeping toward the door, a very guilty look on his face.

"Never mind. Run along."

But he already had.

Warily Colin cast a glance over his bed. Nothing there.

He braced himself and jerked up the covers. Nothing under there, either.

"Hmm."

He leaned over the edge, scoured the floor, stuck his head under the bed. No Houdini. How was that for a disappearing act?

Colin knew the rodent was here somewhere. But after a thorough search of the bedroom, the dresser, the hall, his suitcase, there wasn't a guinea pig to be found. Maybe the kid hadn't been up to something, after all.

He glanced at the clock and groaned. It

was 6:00 a.m., and he was wide-awake.

He heard Julie yelling at the television, something about the number-one answer. Vaguely he remembered a game show with a host who kissed all the women. That English guy from *Hogan's Heroes*. Now there was a job — kissing women on national television and asking them stupid questions for money.

Colin shook his head. If he wasn't careful, he'd know the rules to every game show ever invented and the name of every host. Information like that he could do without.

There was no way he was getting back to sleep, so he stumbled into the bathroom and turned on the shower. He shed his shorts and shirt, then stepped beneath the heated spray.

The thought of Julie's coffee and fresh bakery perked him up, even if he did have to play *Family Feud* to get some.

Colin lathered his hair. Soap dripped into his eyes — and something furry scurried over his toes.

CHAPTER TEN

Marlie had been about to walk out the door with Jake when a thump, followed by a startled cry, made her pause.

She cast a suspicious glance at the boy, who was staring at the ceiling and trying to whistle. "What did you do?"

"Houdini needed a bath."

Marlie dropped her bag and ran up the stairs.

Colin lay in a heap in the hallway. The shampoo in his hair and the long slash of water across the wood floor would have told the tale, even if his being completely naked didn't.

Houdini scrambled out of the bathroom resembling the rat Colin insisted he was — today of the drowned variety. His pink nose twitched in disdain, then he clambered over Colin's back.

Colin leaped to his feet and Marlie got a good look at everything she'd been fantasizing about.

He was gorgeous. Long and lean, with ridges and dips in all the right places. Dark hair swirled across his taut chest, tapering down in an arrow that led directly to . . .

Marlie jerked her gaze away as her face flooded with heat. She'd never seen a naked man. She kind of liked it.

Bending to swipe Houdini off her shoe, Marlie flicked a quick glance through her lashes, but Colin had turned away to snatch a towel from the bathroom. She got a good glimpse of his backside before he whipped the cloth around his waist. His face appeared as red as hers felt.

"Jake strikes again," he muttered.

Even with his lower half covered, he was a sight to see, and Marlie had a hard time focusing on what he was saying. She had to yank her mind from its dizzy interest in his biceps.

What was the matter with her? She'd never been interested in a man's body before. Then again, she'd never been close enough to a man to get interested. Thoughts of sex had always confused her; now thoughts of Colin and sex intrigued her. Too much.

"Uh, sorry," she managed. "What was that about Jake?"

"He likes to sic Houdini on me."

"Sic like a dog?"

"Sure. Your rat-thing hates me."

Marlie laughed. "Houdini can't hate."

"Right. You just keep believing that."

She glanced at the furry animal in her arms. Now that Colin mentioned it, Houdini did appear to be glaring at him.

"When did Jake sic him on you? Besides today?"

Colin shrugged and her mind turned to mush at the sight of his chest muscles bunching. Sheesh, she was behaving like an adolescent with her first boyfriend. Of course the situation wasn't that far off, despite her age and his lack of interest.

"Yesterday he set him on my head when I wasn't paying attention. I'm sure he'll come up with more ingenious plots as the days go by."

"I'll talk to him. Jake doesn't usually misbehave."

"It's all right. I understand where he's coming from."

"You do? Want to share with me?"

"The kid's jealous."

"Of what?"

"Me. For being around you so much."

"But why?"

"You're his first love. He doesn't want any other guy near you. If I were him, I wouldn't, either."

Their gazes met, then his slid away.

What did he mean by that? She wasn't sure how to ask, and he didn't let her.

"You're feeling better?"

"Yes. Thank you."

"I still think you should rest today."

"I'm fine."

If *fine* was being exhausted before she'd even begun and having a stomachache the size of New York City. Nevertheless, if she wasn't contagious and she could stay on her feet, she had to go to work. There was no one else.

"Miss Marlie! Katrina is waiting on the lawn across the street," Jake called from downstairs.

"Oh." Marlie glanced at her watch. "Gotta go. We open at six-thirty."

A lost look crossed his face. "Uh, what should I do?"

"Do?"

"All day?"

"What do you usually do?"

"Go places, meet people, write stuff."

She shrugged. "Do that. I'll be home after five."

"But —"

"Haven't you ever been on vacation?"

"No."

"Never?"

"Have you?"

She couldn't say that she had.

"Guilty," Marlie admitted.

"So what do people do when they have nothing to do?"

"Watch game shows?" She laughed at the face he made. "I thought you were going to send out a few more feelers about Bobby."

"I am. But that'll take me all of an hour. Then I just wait."

"Miss Marlie? Victor's here now, too. There's gonna be trouble."

"Be right down," she called, and turned back to Colin. "Try to relax. See this as a gift. Do all the things you've always wanted to do, but never had time for."

"I can't get to Vietnam and back in a day."

Marlie blinked. "You've always wanted to go to Vietnam? Why?"

"Because it's there."

When she continued to stare at him, he threw up his hands. His towel slipped and he grabbed the edge just before he lost it. *Darn.*

"What would you do if you had too much time on your hands?" he asked.

"Take a walk. Read a book. Feed the birds."

From the expression on his face, her idea

of a vacation was as foreign to him as his was to her.

Colin finished his shower, got dressed, had breakfast. Then he lost at two lightning rounds of *Password* and escaped to his room.

An hour later he'd sent e-mails to everyone in his address book and left messages for several friends and acquaintances. He'd even called and harassed Bobby's superior again, just for fun. Not that it did any good.

"If we'd heard anything, we'd have notified you, Mr. Luchetti."

"What are you doing to find him?"

"All that we can."

"Could I have some specifics?"

"No."

Colin counted to ten as his mother had taught him, then tried again.

"Why not?"

"Because your brother is in the Special Forces, which means he's special."

"No shit," Colin muttered. He hated dealing with the army. They were so freaking literal.

The man cleared his throat. "For all I know, Captain Luchetti could have gone out on an assignment. Looking for him would blow any cover he had."

"You're not looking for him?" Colin shouted.

"We're doing everything we can."

"Why would you tell my mother he's missing if he's out on an assignment?"

"That was a mistake. She should not have been notified."

"When did you plan on notifying her? When you had a body?"

The silence from the other end of the line was all the answer Colin needed. He hung up.

After the useless and frustrating phone call to Afghanistan, Colin had nothing more to do. Annoyed at his dealings with bureaucracy in action, he decided to take Marlie's advice and go for a walk. He'd heard — somewhere — that walking was good for the nerves.

He glanced at his watch and groaned. It was 8:00 a.m. What was he going to do all day? Besides lose his mind.

Ten minutes later Colin strolled down the main street of Wind Lake. He paused at a corner, took in a street sign.

"North Avenue," he read. "How original."

As he wandered down one side, then up the other, the street signs held the same originality. "South Street, East Boulevard, West Way. Hard to get lost, I guess."

He should talk. Back where he came from, half the streets didn't even have names, let alone signs. Farmers were funny that way.

Colin avoided the café. He wasn't hungry, and he liked his face just the way it was.

Wind Lake reminded him a lot of Gainsville. The central avenue was home to the most popular businesses. Wind Lake had the usual gas station, where several old men lifted languid hands in greeting from chairs directly in front.

There was a family-owned grocery store, a drugstore, a hardware store. No coffee shops with fancy lattes or bookstores that doubled as the same. No knickknacks, no lotions and potions. Just plain stuff for just plain folks. Colin had a sudden and nearly undeniable urge to find a mall.

He finished his tour of North Avenue. It was now eight-thirty.

What else had Marlie recommended? Read a book? He didn't have one. There must be a library around here somewhere. Colin shrugged and made a sharp turn on to East Boulevard.

The businesses on the side streets were

less commercial. A real-estate agent, the power company, a lawyer. Colin kept walking. What else did he have to do?

At the end of East Boulevard he paused, looked both ways and crossed the street, though getting hit by a truck would at least put some excitement into his day.

He stepped on to the sidewalk and began to walk back the way he'd come. But a movement behind the windows to his right made him stop. Fascinated, he inched closer, cupped his hands around his face and peered inside.

For a minute he thought he must be staring into a museum. Until he moved back and read the sign above the door.

Wind Lake Weekly News.

Were they serious? Did someone actually print a newspaper on that antiquated equipment? His curiosity aroused, Colin opened the door and stepped inside.

The fragrance of fresh paper and stale coffee assaulted him as soon as he entered. A wave of longing hit him broadside. He rarely went into the offices at the *Dispatch*, but when he did, he relished the scent, the sound, the sight of the thing he loved most in the world — his job.

The *Weekly* had the same smell but none of the noise. The presses were stopped and no one appeared to be home.

Colin examined the machine and its accessories, which took up most of the room. The thing had to be seventy years old. He wondered if it still worked, and if so, how.

"You got business for me, boy?"

Colin, who'd been reaching out to touch, yanked his hand back and spun around. A tiny, wiry man who appeared older than the printing press squinted at him from the doorway.

"I'm sorry?" Colin asked.

"Why? What'd you do?"

He approached with a spry step, running fingers dark with ink through his thinning red hair. He'd obviously been doing that quite a bit already since every strand stuck straight up, giving him a surprised air. The smudges across his forehead lent weight to Colin's assumption.

"I saw your press from outside." Colin waved at the window. "Does it work?"

"Hell, yes, it works. How you think I print the paper every week? Not to mention the stationery orders and such."

From his history-of-the-news class in college, Colin recalled that in the 1920s it was common practice for weekly newspapers to double as specialty-printing shops. On the days the newspaper was not being printed, the workers made office supplies. He'd read that this practice still occurred in some small towns; he just hadn't believed it.

"So you use this press?"

The old man rolled his eyes and snorted. "I don't use a typewriter — at least for the printing. Just for the writing."

"You write on a typewriter?"

"Son, who are you and what do you want?"

"Colin Luchetti." He held out his hand.

The old man shook it and left a good portion of ink behind. "Mickel Sutherland — CEO, managing editor, head writer and chief photographer at the *Wind Lake Weekly*. Most folks just call me Mick. Heard you were in town. Planned to put a mention on page three."

"You're putting me in the paper?"

"Sure. Gotta fill up all that white space somehow. As I understand it, you came searching for your brother. You're staying at the Andersons'. And Garth doesn't like you. Neither does Jake or Ned."

Colin frowned. "You aren't putting that in!"

The old man looked affronted. "You think I'm a gossip? Just-the-Facts Mick, that's what they call me."

"Maybe you should leave me out of the paper altogether."

"Nah. You're the most interesting news we've had since Miss Marlie started writing to that brother of your'n."

"*That* was in the paper?"

"Sure. Did a great little article for Memorial Day."

Colin shook his head. Back home there was the *Gainsville Gazette*, which reported the births, marriages and deaths of the folks therein. Since he'd been more interested in the big picture — namely any other news but the news in his boring hometown — he hadn't read the *Gazette*. The *Weekly* no doubt reported the same kind of trivia. As Mick said, what else would they use to fill up the pages?

"What kind of press is this?" he asked.

"Flatbed. C.B. Cottrell Press, one of the best of its day. My daddy mortgaged everything to buy it. Didn't seem right to retire the thing when it still works just fine."

Colin wanted to see how it worked with a desperation usually reserved for a plum assignment in a country he'd never been to before.

"If you don't mind —" Mick headed across the room toward the desk in the corner, upon which an equally ancient

Smith Corona perched "— I got more work than I can do."

Sitting down, he commenced typing. Colin couldn't remember the last time he'd heard the clack of typewriter keys, instead of the click of a computer keyboard. He stood there a minute and enjoyed it. Until the noise stopped.

"Wanna move along? I need to finish my story on last week's pig-roast fiasco at the Norwegian Club before lunch."

"Uh, sure. Sorry."

Colin let himself out. But as he wandered around town for the next several hours, he was continually drawn to the street on which the *Wind Lake Weekly* sat. Every time he walked past, he heard the clatter of the typewriter keys, and he had a hard time keeping himself from going back inside.

Just as Kurt had predicted, the west wind blew hot that afternoon. Marlie decided it was a good day to fly kites.

She was feeling pretty good, considering. Tired, but she figured running through a field with kites would cure that problem.

The day care looked better than ever. She still couldn't believe Colin had gotten the place cleaned up so fast. Money talked, but that wasn't news to her.

Tiffany hadn't shown up again and hadn't answered Marlie's message as to where she'd been the day before. The girl was fired and Marlie was on her own. Nowhere she hadn't been before.

She always took the children to fly kites in a landlocked area behind the preschool. The owner, Mrs. Anderson, no relation — there were more Andersons in Wind Lake than Kristoffersons — enjoyed watching the children play.

Marlie had hoped the fresh air would revive her, but by the time she got all the kids' kites up, she was dizzy. So she sat down, her own kite resting at her feet.

Times like these were a quandary for her. Marlie adored every child. Their differences, their faults, their strengths made each one unique and special. But times like these also emphasized the loneliness she lived with. She had so many children and none of them were hers.

She wished she were brave enough and rich enough to partake of modern science. She'd read about single women who used artificial insemination to gain the child they coveted. But how would she explain something like that to this town she loved? She didn't think she could, and she wouldn't want her child to be labeled a freak.

Besides, in her dream she had children with the man she loved and shared everything with — her heart, her body, her life. That was as much a part of the dream as the child itself.

A shadow fell over her and she glanced up. The sun sparked off her glasses and she had to close her eyes against the pain that went through her brain like a laser beam.

"Hi," Colin said, and her heart did a nosedive toward her toes.

He flopped next to her in the grass. She didn't know what to say. At the first sound of his voice, an image of him naked flashed behind her closed eyelids.

"Good day?" he asked.

He didn't appear embarrassed that she'd seen all there was to see. Of course, he had a beautiful body. If their positions had been reversed, not only would she be mortified, he'd be disgusted. She wasn't much to look at naked — or rather, she was. Because there was a *lot* of her.

One thing to be said about being a virgin — no one but her mother had ever seen Marlie naked. Hey, there *was* a silver lining to every cloud.

"All days are good," she answered.

"What about yesterday?"

"Great. Until just after noon."

"Is your middle name Pollyanna, by chance?"

"Nope. Inger."

"Whats-er?"

She smiled. "It's Norwegian. Means Ing's daughter."

"Thought you were Martin's daughter."

"Someone at some time must have been Ing's. My gramma's name was Inger Astrid Varner Anderson."

"Quite the mouthful."

"If you like that one, you should stop by the cemetery and read some of the head-stones."

"Excuse me?"

"Haven't you ever done that?"

"No. Ghoulish I'm not."

She shook her head. "What do you do on long Sunday afternoons?"

"Take a plane to somewhere new."

She waited for the punch line, until she realized he wasn't kidding. "Every Sunday you travel?"

"Not every Sunday. But most of them. I like new places."

Marlie didn't understand. She liked her old one.

"When I was a kid," she murmured, "my

parents and I would walk through the cemetery, read the headstones, make up stories about the people buried there. Or if my mom or dad knew them, and they often did, they'd tell stories about their lives. It's a very peaceful pastime."

She could tell from his expression that he thought she was nuts. Which only made two of them. What kind of person went searching for someplace new to start every week?

A person just like her father. She had to remember that or she might just end up watching game shows to keep herself from staring out the window and down the road.

"Miss Marlie, Miss Marlie! Look at me! Look at me!"

Marlie waved at Katrina, whose pink kitty-cat kite trailed a tail of lace. Katrina's kite flew so high it appeared a mere dot against the bright blue sky.

"Isn't it a little late in the year for kite flying?" Colin asked.

"Late?"

"I've always thought March was the time for kites."

"If there's enough breeze, kites are welcome in the sky anytime."

"I never had a kite."

Marlie cast him a quick glance. He stared at the kites dancing together on the breeze with a longing expression. What kind of childhood had he had? No kites, no cemetery tours, and he didn't know how to play kick-the-can.

Maybe that was why he was always on the go. Maybe he was just trying to find a place to call home, which reminded her . . .

"Where do you live?"

"I'm sorry?"

"When you aren't on a plane or in a hotel?"

He shrugged. "Nowhere."

Marlie laughed. "You can't live nowhere. Seriously, where do you get your mail? What's the address on your driver's license?"

"I have my mail sent to the *Dispatch*. My driver's license reads Gainsville, Illinois."

"You really don't have a place of your own?"

"I don't need one."

Marlie couldn't imagine not having a home. But there were a lot of things in Colin's life she found hard to understand.

"Here." She handed him her kite, which had an image of Mary Poppins painted on the front. "Knock yourself out."

The icon brought a smile to his lips. "What if I break it?"

"I've got more."

He stared at the kite, then lifted his gaze to hers. "I'm not sure how."

"I'll show you."

He grinned and the sight made her stomach dance faster than food poisoning. Why did this man affect her the way he did? When he smiled, she wanted to go into his arms and stay there forever. When he frowned, she wanted to take him in her arms and make everything all right. And when he stood before her naked and glistening, she wanted to . . . she wasn't exactly sure.

Colin gained his feet in a lithe movement, then leaned down and held out his hand. She laid her palm against his, and her belly jitterbugged again.

Their gazes met, and something passed between them that Marlie had never experienced before. A sense of rightness — they'd been meant to meet, to touch, to become much more than friends.

He drew her upward as though she weighed no more than the kite in his left hand. Yet when she stood at his side and no longer needed his assistance, he didn't let go.

She was still trapped by his gaze, fascinated by the way his pupils had dilated and reflected a tiny *her* in the center of each. It was as if she were a part of him, as she'd never been a part of anyone else.

Marlie stepped closer. His hand tightened on hers and his head dipped. She caught her breath. The entire world hushed.

Then a voice erupted right behind her. "Oh, no! He's gonna start kissing on her again!"

CHAPTER ELEVEN

Marlie jumped a foot, yanked her hand from his and whirled to face the children. Colin had to clench his fingers to keep from pulling her back.

What was the matter with him? He couldn't stop touching her. No matter how many times he chanted the mantra "brother's girl" or reminded himself that Marlie was a staying kind of woman while he was a going kind of man, he couldn't seem to make his body get the message.

All ten of her kids stood in a line, their kites trailing upward, their lips downward. Jake scowled the hardest — at Colin.

"Go away, kid, you bother me," Colin muttered.

Marlie cast him the evil eye and he shut up. Behind her back, Jake stuck out his tongue. Colin's lips twitched. This was the kind of battle he was used to.

As soon as Marlie took her eyes off him, Colin repaid the favor, lifting his free hand, sticking his thumb in his ear and wiggling his fingers for good measure.

Jake's eyes widened. His mouth dropped

open. He pointed at Colin. "He . . . he —"

"Never mind," Marlie admonished. She glanced at her watch. "We can either go back and wait for your parents at Chasing Rainbows, or you can keep flying your kites. They'll see us over here."

In answer, eight of the children raced off, kites rattling in the wind. Jake continued to gape and point while one little girl shyly approached Marlie. "Ith he your boyfwiend?" she lisped.

"Uh, no."

"Too bad. He'th hot."

Colin choked. Someone had been watching too much prime-time television. The little girl grinned and ran away. Jake snorted, rolled his eyes and stomped after her. Marlie continued to stare at the kites, keeping her back to him.

"Sorry. I don't know where she got that."

"The boyfriend part, or the part where she said I'm hot?"

"Either one."

"I'm not hot?"

"Please. You know you are."

He was ridiculously pleased to hear she thought so. It took some of the sting out of her denying him as a boyfriend, even though he wasn't and never could be.

"Oh, well," he quipped, "kids say the darnedest things."

"Don't they?"

Actually he wouldn't know, but clichés usually got to be clichés for a reason.

Colin rattled the kite. "Ready?"

"What?" She turned. Her gaze went past him. "Mrs. Gunderson, hello. Let me call Katrina."

Marlie moved away, leaving him alone with the Nordic mama. Within minutes, he was surrounded by them. They all seemed to know him, and he hadn't even been in the paper yet.

Mrs. Gunderson, Ms. Larson, Miss Kristofferson and Just-Call-Me Marika all looked alike. Blond-haired, blue-eyed, they were big tall girls who chattered easily with one another and with him, punctuating most of their sentences with the local lingo "Don'tcha know?"

By the time they'd herded their children away, the others had disappeared, as well, even Jake. Colin took a moment to be glad Garth had arrived when he wasn't paying attention.

Marlie stood in the middle of the field, picking up one last kite. He'd heard her telling the children to drop theirs off at Chasing Rainbows when they picked up

their things, but someone must have forgotten.

She appeared a little forlorn, as if she
missed them already. If it were him, he'd
be glad for some peace and quiet.

As he approached, she turned, then
lifted and lowered the kite in her hands.
"Jimmy would forget his head if it wasn't
attached. I worry about him."

Colin wanted to make that sad expression go away. "I used to be the same way.
My brothers, too. My mom despaired of
any one of us ever remembering our stuff
without her around to remind us. I guess I
was always dreaming about exotic lands,
instead of worrying about my gym shoes."

"And now?"

"I don't need gym shoes."

She laughed and his heart lightened. He
wanted to hear her laughter ring out as the
moon turned her skin to alabaster and her
hair trailed over his bare chest. He wanted
to listen to her sigh when he tasted the
soft, sweet skin of her breast. He wanted to
drink his name from her lips when he
made her come.

Colin blinked and the erotic image went
away. Marlie was staring at him. "Where
were you?"

Since he couldn't tell her, he shrugged

and said, "Let's go fly a kite."

Marlie's mom greeted them at the front door, a scowl on her face. "I'm gonna miss *Wheel* if we don't eat quick."

"Sorry, Julie." Colin put his hand on the small of Marlie's back and guided her into the kitchen ahead of him. "We were having fun."

They shared a smile. It *had* been fun. The most Marlie could remember having in years.

Colin truly hadn't known how to fly a kite. She couldn't get over it. After a few fumbled attempts to get his kite up, Marlie had done it for him, running through the grass as the sun dipped low in the sky. Once Mary Poppins was dancing on the wind, she'd turned the string over to him, their fingers brushing in the exchange.

Just that slight touch had made her chest tighten and her breath come faster. His gaze had shifted to her face, then lowered to her mouth before he'd jerked his eyes back to the sky.

Then they'd stood hip to hip, the warm wind in their faces, the sun hot on their hair. They hadn't talked, they'd just been together, and Marlie had felt herself slipping a little bit closer to the edge of a very steep cliff. She couldn't fall in love with him, she just couldn't. He wasn't going to stay.

Her mother had made Swedish meatballs. Everything was on the table. So they dished up and ate, since Julie was fairly twitching with the need to be done in time for *Wheel of Fortune*. Like Pat or Vanna would mind her missing one day.

Marlie set down her fork with an annoyed clatter. She was starting to think about game show hosts the way her mother did — as if they were people she knew. As if they knew her and everything she did. A somewhat creepy trait in her mother, Marlie considered it downright terrifying in herself.

"Thanks for dinner, Mom." She carried her plate to the sink and started the dishes.

As she waited for the water to warm, Marlie stared out the window, but she didn't see the backyard. Instead, she saw her life stretching in front of her. Year after year of other people's children, the only excitement in her life was a brand new game show on network television.

What would happen when her mom passed away? Marlie would be the guinea-pig lady of Wind Lake. Alone in this great big house with a rat-thing or two.

She shook off the depressing thoughts. Where had they come from?

She had a pretty good idea. Having Colin as part of her life right now was making her miss what she'd never had. Marlie sighed and shut off the water.

"You break my heart when you sound like that."

Colin's reflection hovered behind her in the glass. The table was empty, all the dishes on the counter or stacked in Colin's hands. Her mom had snuck off to watch Pat and Vanna. Boy, she *had* gone on a sentimental journey if she'd missed the clatter of plates and her mother's goodbye.

"What's wrong?" he murmured.

She turned and took the dishes from him, then dumped them into the sink. "Nothing."

"Didn't sound like nothing to me. Sounded liked a whole lot of something . . . sad. Anything I can do to help?"

Love me. Marry me. Give me a child.

The words whispered through her mind, but since she could never say them, Marlie merely shook her head and washed the dishes. "You've done enough already."

Confusion creased his forehead. "I haven't done anything except invade your home, nearly put you out of business, not to mention getting your best friend mad at you."

You kissed me, she wanted to add. *You made me want you, need you. Or at least yearn for something I'll never understand.*

"You make it sound like you're a one-man wrecking crew."

"Aren't I?"

He picked up a dish towel and set to drying, just as he had the night before. Once again she was seduced by the normality of the routine, by the connection she already felt to him even though he'd only arrived a few days ago.

"Not at all. It's nice to have you here."

It was a lot more than nice. Something else she could never say.

Someone tapped on the window. Marlie went on tiptoe and looked out. Kurt waved from the other side.

"Time for night games," she murmured.

"We missed them last night."

"We?"

"Well, yeah." His expression turned sheepish. "Can I play?"

Her gaze wandered over his crisp, navy slacks and button-down, oxford shirt. At least he wore tennis shoes, but they were so white they nearly blinded her.

"Maybe you'd better change."

"Don't you love me just the way I am?"

She blinked, opened her mouth, shut it again, uncertain what to say. His teasing smile faded. God, she was such a social reject.

"Never mind." She hurried toward the door. "We need to get out there before a battle erupts over what game to play."

"Wait."

She paused with her hand on the knob. "Yes?"

"I was joking. I'm sorry I made you uncomfortable. Sometimes I forget that not everyone is used to being hassled like I am. In my family, teasing was the only way we knew to show affection. Unless it was punching someone in the gut, and I don't think you're ready for that yet."

He was teasing her again and she snickered. As an only child, she *wasn't* used to such behavior, although she saw enough of it at Chasing Rainbows to get the drift.

"I'll survive," she said.

Even though she really wanted to blurt, *Affection? For me? Wow!*

But that would only make him think her more of a geek than he already did. She was no good at flirting. No good at being casual about the important. Completely inept at pretending she felt something she didn't or the other way around.

Kurt knocked on the door, thank goodness, and she opened it and went on to the porch.

"We wanna play Ghost in the Graveyard," he said.

"Okay."

"What is it with you people and graveyards?" Colin asked.

Marlie glanced over her shoulder. "What's with you and your cell phone?"

His hand went to the appendage at his hip. "Oops."

"Uh-huh."

He plucked the thing from his belt and laid it on the table. "See? I *can* put it away."

Marlie rubbed her hands together. "Which is just what I plan to do to you."

Colin couldn't remember when he'd had more fun. The night was warm. He got all sweaty. He tore his last pair of pants.

And he won.

Chortling and rubbing his palms in an imitation of Marlie's earlier challenge, he followed her back to the house. "Hmm, what do I want?"

She rolled her eyes. "Just pick something, Luchetti, and be done with it."

"But the possibilities are endless."

She cast him a glance he couldn't decipher, especially when the single street lamp sparked rays of light off her glasses and hid her eyes.

"You ever think about getting contacts?"

Her smile froze, and he wanted to smack himself in the forehead with a hammer. "Not that you don't look great with glasses. I just —"

"Yes," she interrupted, "I've thought about contacts. I just can't afford them."

Colin tried to think of something to say and couldn't, so he kept his mouth shut for a change.

"If you want, I'll set you free of your obligation," she said.

"Obligation?"

He couldn't recall having one. Ever.

"To mow my lawn. I can do it."

"No." He shook his head emphatically. "You're not dragging a mower around in this kind of heat, especially when you've been sick. I'll do it."

"Thanks," she murmured, and let them into the house.

His cell phone was jumping about on the kitchen table, vibrating to indicate he had a message pending, as well as ringing periodically to signal the same. He'd never realized how annoying the thing could be. But then, he rarely let his cell phone go unanswered, so the amount of vibrating and rhythmic ringing was kept to a minimum.

He indicated the living room with a flick of his head. "I hope this didn't disturb your mom."

Marlie stepped into the hall. "She's gone to bed."

Colin punched a button and immediately the noise stopped. "Then I hope it didn't keep her up."

"She wears earplugs."

"When she sleeps?"

"My dad snored."

While that shouldn't have made sense, after spending several days with Julie, somehow it did.

Colin pressed in the complicated coordinates necessary to retrieve his messages. Sometimes he felt as if he was operating a NASA spacecraft instead of a cell phone.

His mother's voice filled his ear. "Oh, God, Colin. Where are you?"

Hysteria colored her words. Colin's heart began to beat too fast. This couldn't be good.

"Have you seen the news? A Special Forces operative was captured in Iran.

You've got to find out if that's Bobby. They won't give a name."

She paused as muffled voices spoke to her in the background. "Your dad says you should collect on every favor and promise some of your own. But I'm sure you already have. Let me know what you hear."

She ended the call but not before he heard the tears in her voice. Eleanor Luchetti had cried more in the past year than she had in her entire lifetime.

Colin flipped his phone shut and sat at the table. He forgot all about Marlie until she touched his shoulder. "Bobby?" she asked.

"Yeah."

She left her hand where it was and he was glad. The warmth of her palm, even against his heated skin, felt good — right somehow and comforting. Though he shouldn't let her touch him, he couldn't bring himself to make her to stop.

"Is he . . . ?"

"No. Or at least not yet."

Quickly he told her about his mother's call. She took his hand and led him into the living room. "Let's see what CNN has to say. If they don't know about it, it didn't happen."

He wanted to smile at her sarcasm, but

he couldn't. Marlie retrieved her hand so she could turn on the television. He had to stop himself from reaching for her like a child. As if she sensed his need, she sat next to him on the couch and held his hand in her lap.

It didn't take long for CNN to inform them that his mother's hysteria had been well-founded. Not only was the news anchor saying the same thing in three different ways, but the ticker tape on the bottom of the screen was blaring it, too.

"Must be a slow news day," Marlie remarked.

"Or a very special soldier."

They went silent and listened. There was nothing being reported that Colin didn't already know. He had to find out more. He released Marlie's hand and stood.

"Where are you going?" She reached for him as if afraid he'd walk out of the house and out of her life right that moment.

"I need to make some calls."

"I thought you already called everyone you knew."

"I did."

What was he going to do? Who should he call that he hadn't already? He had no idea.

There was one person who had more

contacts than he did. He hated to ask for a favor, but then, he no longer had a choice. Colin flipped open his phone.

"What?" Gerry answered on the second ring.

"Do you know anything about this soldier who was taken prisoner in Iran?"

"Should I?"

"What can you find out?"

"What do you have that I want?"

With Gerry everything had a price.

"You tell me."

"Next time I tell you to get on a plane for Pyongyang, get on the damn plane."

"That's it?"

"I'm sure I can think of something else. You'll owe me."

Colin hated owing anyone anything — money, favors, information. When he did, what he owed hung over his head like a cloud. Perhaps that was why the idea of a mortgage had always sent him running to another country.

"Fine," he agreed. "I'll owe you."

"I'll see what I can dig up." The line went dead.

"Well?" Marlie asked.

"She'll let me know."

"She?"

Her voice squeaked and he lifted his

head, but nothing was revealed on her face. For a moment there she'd sounded almost jealous.

"My boss. Geraldine Stratton."

"You think she can help?"

"If anyone can, that someone is Gerry."

"You call your boss Gerry?"

"Unless I want to lose a limb. She loathes the name Geraldine."

"Is she . . . ?" Marlie hit the power button on the television remote. Blackness swallowed the screen.

"What?"

"Never mind."

"No, you were going to ask something."

She stared at her hands for several seconds, then blurted, "Is she pretty?"

"Gerry? I never noticed."

"Right. Colin Luchetti didn't notice a woman?"

Well, he'd noticed Gerry. He'd just never thought of her as a woman.

"She's sixty. Over six feet tall and her hair is this long." He held his thumb and forefinger about half an inch apart. "She smokes like a forest fire, drinks her vodka straight and scares the shit out of me."

"Oh!" Marlie blinked. "I guess she ought to be able to beat the information out of someone, then."

A surprised laugh erupted from Colin, ending the panicky inertia he'd been experiencing since he'd heard his mother's voice.

"You know what? I think you're right."

CHAPTER TWELVE

They said good-night at the bottom of the stairs. Marlie hugged him and for the first time since he was five, Colin clung. If this was any other woman, he'd work his wiles, lure her upstairs, seduce her into bed and lose himself in her until dawn.

But this wasn't just any woman. This was Marlie. His brother's girl. Someone he not only respected, but liked.

So he let her go with a squeeze and a brush of his lips across her temple. Even that small, innocent embrace made his body scream for more. He wanted her — no matter who she was, no matter how wrong wanting her might be.

He considered calling his mom back, but it was late and he didn't know anything new. Though he doubted she was asleep, he'd hate to wake her if she was. He'd return the call first thing in the morning.

The night was long. Longer still since heat rose, and there was no air-conditioning in the Anderson home. It had been years since he'd slept in an indoor oven. His parents had no air, either —

cooling huge, drafty farmhouses was expensive — so he had always done his best to avoid the place in the dead of summer.

Colin stripped to his boxers, opened every window, but the wind that had brought the last cry of summer had died.

Lying on his bed, he stared at the lethargic ceiling fan and remembered his brother.

Bobby *was* special. Always had been. Tough, loyal, smart, he could have done anything, but he'd chosen the army. Colin had often called him a class-A idiot to his face, but in his mind Bobby had always been a hero.

"Hell." Colin jackknifed off the bed. "He's not dead. Not yet. So quit preparing his eulogy."

He paced awhile, but that only made sweat roll down his chest like a waterfall. A quick trip to the bathroom, where he doused his head with cold water, helped. But what he really wanted was something icy to drink.

Colin crept downstairs. The silence was so loud it pulsed. When a cricket chirped outside the kitchen window, he jumped, then laughed at himself. What did he expect to find down here? Houdini?

He opened the refrigerator and let out a

sigh at the sight of a pitcher of iced tea. If he knew Julie, this would be the best tea he'd ever tasted, even without the evil heat.

Colin sucked down a glass in a single long gulp, then poured another to take upstairs. The shuffle of a foot against the wood floor made him turn.

The moon turned Marlie's skin to alabaster. Her hair tousled from sleep, she appeared well loved. Her mouth was soft, her breasts swayed enticingly with every movement. The hall light, which she must have turned on when she came out of her room, illuminated her from behind. Her long, cotton nightgown was as sheer as a spiderweb.

Colin swallowed. His mouth had gone dust dry.

She wore white underwear, bikinis, cut high so he could follow the line of her legs all the way up to the V where her thighs met.

Her stomach was a womanly curve, her hips lush, her breasts exquisite. The dark circles of her nipples were silky shadows beneath the material. He ached to lift the nightgown, inch by inch, until he revealed if they were peach, rose or tan, until he could taste first one and then the other.

"I didn't know you were here," she said.

He yanked his gaze from her breasts to her face. She was staring at his chest. He remembered he was wearing little more than a swimming suit. And from the way his body throbbed . . .

Spinning around, he busied himself putting the pitcher of iced tea back into the refrigerator. Maybe if he let the cool air hit him below the waist — for about an hour — he'd be ready to face her again.

"I was thirsty."

An inane comment, but the only one he had.

"Me, too."

She glided close and reached past him. Her hair brushed his bicep, and he clenched his teeth so hard his jaw crackled.

She cast him a quick glance. Her cheeks weren't red. She obviously had no idea he'd been able to see everything beneath her gown.

While Marlie poured her own tea, he escaped into the shadows of the kitchen where he hoped his reaction would be invisible to the naked eye. Or at least her naked eye, since she wasn't wearing her glasses.

Marlie shut the refrigerator and the room darkened. The hall light splashed a yellow rectangle across the vinyl floor.

Both of them stood beyond its reach.

He listened to her swallow, the sound soothing, familiar — as she was. How could he feel as if he'd known her always when he hadn't been aware she existed until just this week?

She set her empty glass next to the full one he'd forgotten. "You couldn't sleep."

She wasn't asking, but he answered, anyway. Anything to keep his mind off the rock-hard implement in his shorts that seemed to have a mind of its own and no conscience whatsoever.

"No." He leaned against the counter, let his hands fall loosely in front of him in a gesture he hoped appeared casual. "I keep remembering things about Bobby. Then I find myself thinking of him in the past tense and —"

"It's normal to think like that."

"Is it? Then why do I feel as if I'm burying him alive?"

Silence fell between them, broken only by the annoyingly chipper cricket outside.

"Thinking something doesn't make it true."

Which was lucky for him, because he'd already thought of having sex with her about a hundred times. His erection leaped against his hand, and he resisted the urge to slap himself. He was as bad as a dog that couldn't stop humping any leg in the vicinity.

"You're doing everything you can. I know it's not easy being patient. Especially for a man like you."

He lifted his head. A ghost of white against the navy blue night, she looked almost virginal.

He coughed. *Hell.* What if she was?

"Here."

She crossed the room with his neglected glass in her hand. Panic flared. If she got too close, he wasn't sure what he might do.

"No." He waved both hands, shook his head. But talking only made him cough more.

"Shh."

She patted his shoulder, then left her hand there to steady him as she brought the rim to his lips. He had no choice but to take a sip.

The tea soothed his throat. Her nearness was anything but soothing. She leaned across him to set the glass on the counter, and her palm slid from his shoulder to his forearm as her stomach brushed him in the worst-possible place. Or maybe it was the best.

She froze, then lifted her gaze to his. A

woman's knowledge filled her eyes and she tilted her head.

"Colin?" she whispered.

A man could only take so much temptation. His hands moved of their own accord to her waist. He yanked her tightly against his body. Her eyes went wide and her mouth opened. Which worked well for him. He dived right inside.

Her lips were cool, her skin fiery hot. Her tongue tasted of tea. He kissed her as if she was the only thing keeping him sane, and right now she was. Their embrace the only anchor in a world that no longer had any meaning.

No gentleness now, no leisurely exploration. He wanted her, hard and fast. Right here. On the counter, the table, the floor.

Her fingers tightened, pulling him closer. Her mouth opened wider, her tongue acrobatic, enticing him to fill his hands with the soft flesh of her breasts.

She sighed in pleasure when he kneaded them, thumbing her nipples, then rolling them between two fingers.

He'd never touched breasts this big and this real. If he died right now, he'd go to hell happy.

She smoothed her palms across his chest, stroking his skin, making him ache.

He couldn't think. All he could do was want. Her, them, this.

Trailing a line from her eager lips to the curve of her neck, he took a fold of her skin between his teeth and suckled.

Gasping, she tangled her fingers in his hair and murmured his name.

The word brought back a semblance of sanity. He was *Colin.* Colin *Luchetti.* And this woman whose breasts he held in his hands? That would be his *brother's* girl.

He yanked his fingers and his mouth from her skin.

Yep, he was definitely going to hell.

Her eyes opened, her gaze unfocused. "Did I do something wrong?"

His hands on her shoulders, he inched her away. She resisted, but he was stronger than she was. "It isn't you. It's me."

"What about you?"

Colin escaped to the far side of the room where he wouldn't be tempted to touch her again. But the second he looked at her, he knew he could go to Botswana and still be tempted.

He spun around and stared out the window. "I shouldn't have done that."

"Why not? We're over twenty-one and I'm not complaining."

Colin drew in a long, hot breath of night.

"You're my brother's girl."

"I'm what?"

"Bobby's. He loves you."

She laughed. "Where did you get this?"

"His letter."

"I seem to have missed the part where he declared his everlasting love."

"He said you were the best thing that ever happened to him."

"And that's secret Luchetti lingo for 'I love you'?"

"Close enough," he muttered.

In his family the L-word wasn't used much. They showed each other, instead. His dad hadn't actually told his mom he loved her until they'd been married more than thirty years. Even Colin had to admit that was pushing it.

He'd never said the word to anyone but his mother. Wasn't sure how. Obviously Bobby wasn't sure how, either.

"You guys are nuts."

"Well, we *are* guys."

She snorted. "You won't touch me because I'm Bobby's, yet I've never met the man."

She sounded really pissed, so he turned. She'd crossed her arms over her chest and began tapping her foot. Uh-oh, he knew that pose from a lifetime with his mother.

"Brothers have a code," he hastened to explain. "It's unwritten but also unbreakable."

"Let me guess — never touch your brother's girl."

"That would be the one."

"Even if she touches you first?"

He sighed. "Especially then."

Marlie returned to her hot, lonely room. She got in bed, then she got back out. She walked around, kicked the laundry basket, considered punching a pillow. She'd never been so angry in her life.

"Did anyone think to ask me whose girl I wanted to be?" she asked the room.

In midpace, Marlie paused. An excellent point. Even if Bobby did love her, and she had a hard time believing he did, she didn't love him.

So she'd fantasized about him. That wasn't a crime or a commitment. No matter what the Luchetti family code said.

She blew a derisive burst of air past her lips. "Sounds more like the Luchetti family curse to me. I thought modern men were able to say 'I love you'."

As if she knew one damn thing about modern men.

The floorboards above her head creaked.

She lifted her eyes. He was pacing, just as she had been.

For the same reason? Did he regret having pushed her away? Or was he agonizing still over holding her close in the first place?

Marlie lay back down and stared at her ceiling fan. It did little to cool the turgid heat of the room. She began to count the revolutions, hoping the repetition would cause her to drift off. An hour later, she was still awake, and the floorboards upstairs still creaked.

She couldn't stay here any longer. There was something she had to say.

Marlie hurried through the house on silent, bare feet. She took the steps at a run, not slowing down until she stood outside his door.

Then she just stood there. She couldn't make herself knock. Her heart thundered so loudly she could no longer hear his footsteps. Maybe he'd finally gone to bed. If so, she didn't want to wake him. Marlie chewed on her thumbnail, a bad habit she thought she'd broken long ago.

The door swung open. His skin shone silver in the ray of moonlight spilling through the window and across the floor. He was both beautiful and masculine, an enticing combination of curves and angles.

He didn't say a word, just stood beneath the light of the moon and waited.

"I . . . I wanted to say something."

"Say it."

His voice was a whisper. And his face a mere shadow in the night.

"You never asked me if I love him."

She held her breath through several chirps of the cricket. At last he spoke. "Do you?"

"No." She swallowed and plunged ahead. "I'm not in love with *Bobby.*"

Colin moved closer, until the moonlight trickled over his face. "What's that supposed to mean?"

She wasn't sure. Could she love Colin when she'd only known him a few days? Why not? He'd believed his brother was in love with her, and she'd never been within a hundred miles of the man.

Marlie stepped over the threshold. She'd come here for one thing. Him. And she didn't mean to leave until she got it.

"I'm a twenty-five-year-old preschool teacher, and that's the bottom of the barrel. I've never felt for anyone what I feel for you."

When he opened his mouth, she held up her hand. "Don't say it's too soon. I've been telling myself that for hours. If you don't feel the same way, say so and I'll leave. But if you do . . . Don't let what you think Bobby *might* have meant or *might* have felt stop us from having . . . whatever it is we could have."

He didn't move, or speak, or throw himself at her feet and beg to be her lover. Why was she not surprised?

"Marlie, I —"

Before he said something they'd both regret, she interrupted. "I don't *want* to be Bobby's girl."

"No?"

"No." The cricket chirped — once, twice, a thousand times. "I want to be yours."

He crossed the short distance still separating them and touched his knuckles to her cheek with such tenderness her eyes teared. He was going to turn her down, and then she'd never be able to look him in the face again.

Worse, she'd never understand all the questions her body had been shouting since he'd first kissed her what seemed like a lifetime ago.

"Marlie?" he murmured.

She sighed and hung her head. "Yes?"

"I want you to be mine, too."

CHAPTER THIRTEEN

Marlie lifted her head so fast she nearly clipped Colin in the nose. He reared back.

"Whoa." He laughed. "Take it easy."

"Wh-what are you saying?" she asked.

He took her hand, drew her closer, then tucked her against his body and slowly shut the door. "You know exactly what I'm saying. Marlie, may I kiss you?"

The echo of the children's game, Mother May I, which they'd played a few hours ago, made her smile, then lift her mouth.

"You may," she whispered seconds before his lips claimed hers.

The kiss was a combination of their first and their second — both gentle and rough — with the promise of so much more to come.

Marlie clung to him as he brought to life all the wonderful feelings, the thrilling questions. Knowing that soon the answers would be hers made their embrace the most exciting she'd ever known.

Before she could start to analyze how pathetic that was, Marlie ran her fingertips over his chest, and when he moaned into her mouth, then grasped her hips and yanked her nearer, she forgot her sexual ineptitude. A wave of lust washed over her, so strong her knees shook. She wanted this man more than she'd ever wanted anything.

He ended the kiss with a hug and a tiny peck at the corner of her mouth. "You're trembling," he murmured. "Maybe we should —"

She went up on tiptoe and kissed him again. Mouth open, tongue searching, she practiced everything he'd taught her about seduction in the few short embraces they'd shared. Lifting her mouth until it was a mere breath from his, she said, "We should. Definitely."

His lips curved and hers did the same. But when he bent and lifted her into his arms, she let out a tiny shriek. "Colin, put me down!"

He ignored her plea, nuzzling her neck as he crossed to the bed.

He was so long and lean, she hadn't comprehended how much bigger than her he was. Marlie always felt like a moose around any other man but Garth. Yet Colin carried her as if she weighed little more than a child.

He treated her gently, too, as he lowered

her to the single bed and covered her body with his.

Though the room was stifling, she didn't mind the heat of his skin against hers. For the first time the cold, lonely place deep inside of her warmed.

They fit each other like a puzzle. His ridges to her valleys, her curves to his sharp planes. She'd never considered how a man's body and a woman's could be so different, yet come together in complete harmony.

His forearms flexed on either side of her head as he pressed featherlight kisses across her face. The pressure of his mouth deepened as the kisses strayed to her neck.

Her fingers twined in his hair. When he nuzzled the fullness of her breasts where they strained against her worn cotton bodice, her hands clenched and urged him on.

His lips closed over an aching nipple, sucking both her and her gown into his mouth in a single, hard thrust. His tongue rolled the nipple against his teeth, tugging, arousing, making her gasp.

He leaned on one arm, the movement pressing his lower body more firmly against hers. Shiny white lights danced in front of her eyes. Something wonderful lay beyond those lights, something she wanted to see right now.

She moved her hips and he muttered something unintelligible as he grabbed her waist. "Hold on, honey. You'll put an end to this before we even get started."

She thought things were going pretty well, but then, she didn't know where they were going. So she stilled and let him show her the way.

"The first time I saw you," he said, "all I could think about was touching your skin."

Holding her gaze, he slipped loose button after button until the gown lay open to the waist. Callused fingertips slid along the swell of her breast. His palm cupped, then lifted the weight.

"I knew you'd be softer than anything I'd ever touched."

He shifted and sat up. The loss of his warmth, even in the incredible heat of the night, made her cold and lonely.

"Wait," she began, but he was already reaching for her again.

"Let me see you, Marlie." He flicked a finger at her gown. "Will you take that off?"

She didn't want to, but how could she refuse? Even she knew this was done without clothes. At least the room was dark, though right now she cursed the bright and shiny moon.

A deep breath gathered her courage. She sat up, then whipped the gown over her head and tossed it aside. Lying back down, she stared at the ceiling.

She knew what he'd see. A big girl — large breasts with blue veins that marred the too-white skin. Big thighs, wide hips, curved stomach. She was glad he couldn't see the size of her butt. He'd likely run screaming from the room, the house, her life.

She started at the light stroke of his fingertip across her stomach. "I knew you'd be beautiful," he whispered, and her startled gaze shot to his face.

He was serious — or at least a very good actor.

She frowned. "I'm not —"

He laid his hand flat against her belly. The movement stopped her in mid-denial. "You are. Soft, round, feminine. You're everything a woman should be. I could look at you forever."

Lowering his head, he pressed his mouth where his hand had been.

She wasn't sure what to make of his words. All her life her mother had told her she was a big girl — like her dad. Of course, her mom was the size of a mosquito.

When Marlie despaired about the size of her thighs, Julie had shrugged and said, "Blood will tell. Your dad has legs like a tree trunk."

To a teenage girl, tree-trunk legs were not attractive, even if they were just like her dad's.

All thoughts fled when Colin's mouth strayed upward and his lips repeated their earlier performance, sans the cotton nightdress. His tongue sampled first one nipple, then the other, teasing, tormenting, until she was squirming against the bed, against him.

"Colin," she begged. "Please."

"Hush, honey. I'll make it better. You'll see."

But he didn't make it better, or maybe he did. She couldn't decide, because she couldn't think. He ran his hands all over her body, followed their path with his mouth. Slid his fingertips beneath the elastic of her panties, then found the throbbing center of her body with his thumb and pressed.

She arched up off the bed and he held her, rode the explosion with her, murmuring "Marlie" against her hair.

229

As soon as she could breathe again, think again, she felt the hard, firm length of him and knew they weren't finished yet. Shocking herself with her own boldness, she reached between them and stroked him as he had stroked her.

His breath caught and his hand flew to her wrist. She lifted her gaze. "I want you, Colin. I thought you understood that."

"It's a bad idea. You . . . you're . . . uh . . . Well, at least I think you are."

"A virgin? Yes, but that doesn't mean I want to die that way."

She startled a laugh out of him, but he still held on to her hand. "We shouldn't."

"If I had a dime for everything I shouldn't do that I've done . . ."

"You'd probably have a dime."

He knew her so well.

"Please."

Though he held her wrist tightly, she could still move her fingers, so she did. Molding, stroking, seducing, she hoped. From the expression on his face, she was winning whatever battle he waged.

"Life's too short," she murmured. "Who knows what will happen tomorrow? I've had a lot of regrets. But this night won't be one of them. Unless you make me leave before you show me everything I've missed."

He was shaking his head no, even as he released her hand and met her lips with his.

He was hard against her fingers, trembling in her arms, and his tongue went wild. Moments later he yanked her panties away, tossing them to join his boxers in a heap on the floor.

She fell back on the bed, taking him with her. They fit together again, just as they had before. And right when she thought the mystery was about to be solved, he tensed and leaped away cursing.

"What? What did I do?"

"Nothing. It's not you. I'm an idiot. I . . . Just wait a minute."

He left her, and she wanted to shriek as her body throbbed for his. He bent over his suitcase, rustled around, and finally she understood what he was after.

She was as much of an idiot as he was. Though she could plead ignorance of proper condom procedure, ignorance was a poor excuse when staring an unplanned pregnancy or a lovely STD in the face.

How was that for a romance killer?

"Sorry." He returned and tugged her close. "When I'm with you I forget every promise I ever made, even to myself."

The sadness in his voice caused her heart to flutter. She didn't want him to think about codes or rules or brothers. Not now.

"Shh," she whispered, and touched his face. "Forget some more with me."

The moon had slipped below the horizon, bathing the room in darkness. The night held its breath and so did she.

His eyes glittered. His arms tightened. His weight pressed her into the mattress, and soon neither one of them remembered anything but each other.

She understood the mechanics; she knew it would hurt the first time. Still she tensed at the sharp pain, and he stilled.

"I'm sorry," he repeated. "I don't want to hurt you."

She had a feeling he wasn't just talking about this moment.

Despite her rising passion, which had returned as soon as the pain faded, she also felt the need to soothe and comfort him. It was her nature.

Her hands moved along his shoulders and spine, stroking and arousing. She pressed against his lower back, drawing him more deeply into her.

"I'm yours now," she whispered. "Don't apologize for giving me what I wanted."

He didn't answer; his body began to move against her, within her. He buried his face in her hair, lifted her hips and showed her with long, firm strokes that she was truly his, and she always would be.

Something furry crawled across his belly.

Colin awoke with a start and very nearly leaped out of bed before he realized it was Marlie's hair that was giving him guinea pig nightmares.

He stilled, afraid he'd wake her, though the gray light through the windowpane revealed dawn was on the way. He'd have to get up soon enough. He didn't relish being caught like this by her mother.

Julie seemed a harmless nut, but he wouldn't put it past the woman to have a shotgun around here somewhere.

Colin shuddered. What had he done?

Taken Marlie's virginity. Made promises he doubted he could keep. To a girl like her, what they'd shared meant forever, and Colin Luchetti wasn't a forever kind of guy.

Bobby was going to kill him for touching her; he'd kill him slowly if Colin broke her heart, too. But he wasn't sure how to avoid it.

She shifted and her breath brushed his

skin. His body sprang to attention and he started to count baby sheep — the only way he'd ever found for diverting his attention from sex. To him lambs were the ultimate in innocence, kind of like Marlie herself. When he thought of them, he couldn't think of sex.

He reached 120 lambs before he could concentrate on anything other than flipping her onto her back and waking her up the best way he knew how.

Hell, he should've packed his bags and run like the coward he was the second she appeared at his door.

But it had already been too late. He'd been a goner from the first time he saw her face. The instant he'd heard her laughter he was hooked.

She was sunshine in a world of shadow. Wherever he went he found darkness and doom. What did they have in common besides . . . this?

He wasn't sure. But he knew he hadn't been happy in a long time, and even though he felt as if he'd betrayed his brother, he couldn't give her up. Not yet.

Sooner or later he'd leave. Leaving was what he did best. She had to know that, and if she'd forgotten, he'd remind her.

But until then, where was the harm in

enjoying each other? The damage had already been done.

Colin glanced at the window where the light had gone from gray to pink. He kissed Marlie's brow, tugged on her ear. "Hey, sleepyhead. Time to get up."

She awoke with a smile. Her eyes still closed, she murmured, "Colin," and unerringly found his mouth. For yesterday's virgin, she did pretty well.

And suddenly he was counting sheep again.

Colin managed to get Marlie out of his room before her mother woke up. Why did he feel as if he were in high school again?

Not that he'd ever snuck a girl out of his room in the dawn's early light. His mother had the ears of a bat and the nose of a bloodhound. Nothing got by that woman.

Which was why he wasn't surprised at her phone call while he was still dripping from the shower.

"What are you up to?" she demanded.

He nearly dropped the phone. How could she know? She wasn't even here.

"I . . . I . . . Up to? Nothing."

"Hmm. I doubt that. What have you done about your brother?"

Colin pulled himself together. His

mother wanted to know about Bobby and what he'd learned. Not about Marlie and what he'd done.

Quickly he filled her in, which was very quick, because he hadn't discovered anything new.

"Do you think Gerry can help?"

"I know she can."

He also knew he'd pay for it, but he'd do so gladly if Bobby got home alive.

"Will you be coming to the farm soon?"

"No."

He answered without thought, then stood blinking into the bathroom mirror. Even though he doubted Bobby was going to show up in Wind Lake, he wasn't leaving. He couldn't. Not yet.

His mother sighed. "Fine. I guess I'm not surprised. You never did like it here."

"Mom." She was queen of the guilt trip — just like any mother he'd ever met. Colin had always suspected guilt-inducement pills were given out in the disguise of prenatal vitamins. "It's not that I don't like it there."

"But you don't."

He stifled a sigh. "You're right, I don't. But that has nothing to do with you. I love you."

"You just don't love the farm."

"Do I have to?"

She laughed. "No. Dean loves it enough for all of you."

His brother's adoration of all things bovine had saved Colin and his other brothers from a lifetime of drudgery. The best part was Dean saw farming as his own personal heaven.

"I'll come home eventually. I always do."

"I know. I just miss my boy."

He smiled. "You've got four more."

"That's right. I *don't* need you," she teased.

She sounded better this morning. No longer hysterical, and that set his mind at ease. Sure she was upset, but she wasn't going to show it. Not Eleanor Luchetti. She was the family's rock and she always had been.

"How's Marlie?"

"Why do you want to know?"

Too quick, too defensive. He'd blown any chance he had of pleading innocent.

"Hmm," she said again. "Better be careful."

"I always am," he said.

His mother's snort doubled as an opinion and a goodbye.

By the time he made it downstairs, Marlie was gone. That didn't surprise him.

His missing her did. He considered a visit to Chasing Rainbows, but figured that would appear too needy and pathetic. Besides, he'd had enough kid time to last a lifetime.

Julie was already engrossed in an outdated version of *Let's Make a Deal*. Colin considered joining her, until she threw her shoe at the television and shouted, "Not that door! There's an ass back there, you ass."

A quick trip to town was in order. Especially since he was fresh out of pants. If he hadn't brought along his running shorts, he'd be down to his boxers. He had no doubt that, in Wind Lake, waltzing around in his underwear would land him in Chief Moose's jail.

As it was, he felt uncomfortable in his shiny red shorts. He'd bought them so he would stand out jogging on the side of the road. He'd heard too many horror stories of runners being picked off by inattentive drivers. So far the shorts had done their job. But right now, on the streets of Wind Lake, people were staring.

He ducked into the first store he found. Gunderson's seemed to have a little bit of everything. *Thank you, God.* Colin hurried to the men's section. No silk slacks. Oh, well, he'd only ruin them.

The selection consisted of blue jeans and heavy-duty work pants. Considering the heat, he gave the work pants a pass, but he couldn't find any jeans in his size. Did everyone in town wear a size forty-inch waist and above?

"Whatcha doin?"

Colin spun about to discover Katrina studying him from behind a pile of striped overalls. Today she wore pants, instead of a dress, but she was still a fashion icon.

Her red polka-dot slacks ended at midcalf to show off her white lace anklets and red Keds. Her matching top belled out as she spun round and round until she stumbled and nearly fell. Her hair was held back from her face with a polka-dot head-band. She really was adorable — if you were into that sort of thing.

When she regained her balance, she peered up at him, waiting.

"Oh . . . uh, I need slacks. But I can't find my size."

"You're skinny. Mommy said."

Colin recalled meeting Mrs. Gunderson during kite-flying exercises. Since she stood as tall as he did and outweighed him by fifty pounds, he understood her point of view.

"Are there any other pants around?"

"You could try these." She placed a tiny hand on top of the stack of blue-and-white-striped overalls. Her fingernails were painted neon-red.

Just the sight of those monstrosities made Colin smell manure. His dad wore them in the winter. Colin had sworn never to do so himself.

"No, thanks."

Katrina shrugged, unconcerned. If he had a wardrobe like hers, he'd have no worries, either. But since he lived out of a suitcase, he traveled light, buying what he needed when he needed it. He'd never encountered a place where he couldn't acquire his heart's desire in the nearest mall.

"Some daddies wear stretchy straps if their pants are too big." She lifted a pair of suspenders.

Daddies? He cringed, shook his head. "How about a belt?"

She pointed to a nearby table. The tangled jumble of leather, both black and brown, reminded Colin of a bed of snakes. He rooted through them, anyway, found the smallest size — also a forty. This wasn't going to work.

"Any other place to buy clothes around here?"

"Nope. Mommy says we're the monopoly at Wind Lake." Her tiny face creased into a confused frown. "But I never see any of that pretty colored money or Marvin Gardens around here."

Colin laughed. "I bet not."

So Gunderson's had the monopoly on clothes. Too bad for him. He'd just have to make do. He chose the smallest pair of jeans and the least gaudy suspenders he could find, which were maroon with gold stripes.

"Golden Gophers," Katrina stated.

Could that be a child's version of son of a —

"Pardon me?"

"Those are Gopher colors." She held up the purple-and-yellow suspenders Colin had discarded. "I like Viking colors better."

"Ah."

Not a made-up curse word, but the state university mascot. The suspenders he'd chosen had the colors of the University of Minnesota. Now that he looked, every pair of suspenders represented a Minnesota sports team. What were the odds that he'd chosen the colors that represented a furry rodent?

He shouldn't be surprised at the obsession with team spirit. Sometimes he swore that everything in Illinois was blue and orange in the fall or red and black in the winter. He'd thought Minnesotans might have more sense.

From the selection of T-shirts, he'd thought wrong. Once again Colin had the scintillating choice between Gopher gold, Viking purple and Twins red, white and blue.

"Decisions, decisions," he muttered, settling once again with the Gophers as the least gaudy offering available, despite the rodent issue.

He made his purchases and changed in the dressing room, stuffing his running shorts into the shopping bag. He'd thought Katrina had run along to school, but when he stepped out, there she was.

He twirled as she had done. Lucky he had the suspenders or he'd have lost his pants. At that rate, Chief Moose would have no trouble finding grounds to lock him away forever.

"What do you think?" he asked.

Katrina gave a decisive nod. "*Now* you fit in."

She skipped off, leaving him staring after her as panic fluttered to life in his stomach.

He fit in?

Here?

CHAPTER FOURTEEN

Marlie was singing as she opened the door of Chasing Rainbows. Her song turned into a screech when a huge shadow separated from the others in the room.

"Garth! You nearly gave me heart failure." She opened the shades and morning sunlight spread across the freshly cleaned carpet. Funny how the whole world looked brighter this morning. "Where's Jake?"

"With Ned."

She raised an eyebrow. "There is no Ned."

"Really? Then how come it seems like there is?"

Marlie laughed, but Garth didn't join her. Something was wrong.

"Is Jake okay?" Panic clutched at her chest. She reached for Garth's hand. His huge paw enveloped hers.

"He's fine. Relax. I left him eating pancakes at the café. I wanted to talk to you. Alone."

Able to breathe again, Marlie disengaged her fingers from his and strode toward the office so she could set down her bag. Garth followed.

"The bed-wetting seems to be better." Marlie plopped into her chair. "There hasn't been a problem here lately. How's he been at home?"

"Fine."

Impatience sharpened his voice, which wasn't like Garth. Her unease deepened.

"I didn't come here to talk about Jake."

"I told you, Ned will go away when he's good and ready and not before."

"I don't want to talk about Ned, either."

Marlie spread her hands and shrugged. "What, then?"

"I want to talk about us."

She blinked. "Us?"

His pale Nordic skin flushed just as hers always did, and he stared at his feet as he hovered in the doorway. "Jake loves you," he said.

"And I love Jake."

"He needs a mom."

"He has you."

He took a deep breath and blurted, "I want you to be his mom, Marlie."

She sat there for several ticks of the clock, trying to make sense out of his words. She couldn't.

"You lost me."

"I'm afraid I did."

He lumbered across the room, taking the seat on the other side of the desk. Then he lifted his dark, sad eyes to hers. "I didn't realize what I had until he came."

"He, who?"

"Luchetti."

"Colin? What does he have to do with anything?"

"Everything. Marry me, Marlie. Give my little boy a mother."

"Huh?"

She'd imagined many marriage proposals in the lonely quiet of her room. But never one from her best friend. And never one where her answer was "Huh?"

Garth leaned forward. "We can be a family. You, me and Jake. Your mom, too. Jake would be good for her."

She couldn't think of anything to say, so she said nothing. Garth didn't have the same problem.

"Jake needs you, Marlie. I need you. Please, say yes."

"Garth." She shook her head, then stood and moved to Houdini's cage — empty again, doggone it — because she couldn't sit still. "You aren't making any sense."

"I'm making the most sense I've made in a long time. We care about each other. I don't want to be alone anymore. You want a family. I've got one."

"I want love, too."

"I love you."

"That's not the kind of love I mean."

"You think *he* loves you?"

Marlie winced at the blunt question, then answered with equal bluntness. "No."

She moved as far away from Garth as the small room would allow. Her bright and shiny morning had sprung a cloud.

What she and Colin had shared had been life-changing, earth-shattering. *For her.* For him it had no doubt been another in a long line of one-night stands. Garth was right. Colin didn't love her, but she'd never believed he did.

She sensed Garth's approach. Gently he turned her to face him. Earnestness tightened his features. "I'll give you your dream, Marlie. Love, home, a family."

"What about children?" The words slipped out.

His eyes widened. His cheeks flushed again. Then he kissed her before she could take the words back.

In all their years as friends, they had never kissed on the lips. Why would they?

Marlie closed her eyes and tried to respond. Garth was a good kisser. He was well-versed in the basics and he had a few tantalizing variations of his own.

However, the only thing she felt while kissing him was . . . silly. She had to run through her multiplication tables to keep from laughing. She didn't think Garth would find this funny.

He lifted his head. Their eyes met and together they shrugged.

Garth let her go. "I've had sex with women I like a lot less than you, Peanut."

"Too much sharing," she muttered.

"Sorry." He backed away as his gaze held hers. "We can make it work. I know we can."

She shook her head, but he lifted one huge hand in a staying motion. "Just think about it. Don't say no yet."

"Garth —"

"He isn't going to stay. You know it. I know it. He knows it." Garth paused, considered a moment, then plunged ahead. "You always told me you didn't want the same life your mother had. Waiting, hoping, watching and someday finding out that he isn't coming back — like your dad."

Marlie flinched and Garth sighed. "I'm sorry. I don't mean to hurt you, but you have to know that there's no future with a guy like that."

She hadn't planned on a future. She'd just wanted to have a past, some memories, a life for crying out loud, but she wasn't going to tell Garth that.

He opened his mouth to say something else, but the thunder of little feet stopped him.

Jake skidded into the room with Katrina on his heels. "Hi, Dad. Hi, Miss Marlie. There he goes!"

The two of them fell to their knees and started crawling around on the floor like manic dogs. Houdini shot from behind the filing cabinet, and the chase was on. When Marlie looked up, Garth was gone.

Which was probably for the best. She didn't want to hurt his feelings, but what *had* he been thinking?

Just because she wanted marriage, family, children didn't mean she'd marry someone she didn't love and make babies with him. The very idea . . .

She shuddered. Perhaps yesterday she might have agreed, or at least considered the offer. But after making love with Colin, she couldn't.

What they'd shared had been special, magic. She wanted to share with him again. Soon. She was probably falling in love with him, if she wasn't there already.

She was going to get her heart crushed and handed back to her in teenie-tiny pieces.

"And right now, I couldn't care less," she muttered.

"What?" Jake stuck his head around the doorjamb.

"Never mind." She waved her hand in a shooing gesture. "Just find the rat-thing."

" 'Kay."

He disappeared and soon several other childish voices drifted to her from the outer room. They should have Houdini cornered.

In a few hours.

Colin was walking back to the Anderson home, wondering what he was going to do all day while he waited for Gerry's call, or anyone else's, when suddenly he glanced up. His feet had led him to the *Wind Lake Weekly*.

Why he was so fascinated with the place, he wasn't sure. Maybe it was dementia brought on by mind-numbing boredom.

He couldn't recall the last time he'd had nothing to do and nowhere to be. He didn't like it.

The door opened and Mick's red head popped out. "Nice threads," he said.

Colin wasn't sure if Mick was being sarcastic or not. He chose the latter. "Thanks."

"Perfect for what I have in mind. Get in here."

The door slammed behind him. Colin stood there a few seconds, then scrambled for the entrance.

Mick's printing press was humming — make that thumping. The scent of ink and new paper filled the air. Heat radiated from the machine in stifling waves.

"Pre-Labor Day circular," Mick shouted above the din. "Has to go out tomorrow."

Colin nodded. His gaze was captured by the printing press. He found himself hypnotized by the rhythmic movements.

The old man fed sheets in from the front, two at a time. When these were done, he refed them so they could be printed on the back. Then they went into the folder. His movements were as rhythmic as those of the machine.

"Hey!" Mick yelled right in his ear.

Colin jumped a foot off the ground and clapped his hand over his ringing eardrum.

"Hey what?" he returned.

"You like my machine, don't you?"

"Yeah."

"Wanna play with it?"

Colin returned his gaze to the pumping press. "Uhhuh."

"Great. You're hired."

"I didn't know I applied."

"You did. I'm not getting any younger. And my circulation is up."

"To what?"

"Two hundred and twenty."

Hardly seemed worth the trouble, but then again, how could Mick possibly print and fold any more than that? It must take him days as it was.

"Twenty hours a week and I can't pay you," Mick continued.

Colin grinned. "Now there's an offer I can't refuse."

Five hours later he was glad he hadn't. He'd been a journalist for eight years, but he'd never understood what it took to create a newspaper from the ground up. Of course, the process was quite a bit different from the one used at the *Chicago Dispatch*.

Gerry had installed a KBA Commander press just last year. Considering the *Dispatch* produced multiple color pages and had a circulation in the hundreds of thousands, Colin couldn't believe she'd waited so long to computerize.

At the *Weekly*, Mick still did typesetting

at a keyboard. He had a make-up bench for assembling copy and advertising, and a proof press to check everything over before feeding it into the flatbed press. Colin worked like a dog and had the time of his life.

Mick knew stories that would curl a man's toes. He reminded Colin of Gerry. Newsprint in his blood, tall tales coming out of his mouth.

"And then Kirby Puckett hit that ball so hard I swear the stuffing flew out of it."

Mick placed another stack of the finished product in the back room, preparatory to its being loaded into a delivery truck by a gullible high school student, who actually did get paid, but not much.

"We'll never know because they never found that ball," Mick continued. "Heard tell someone picked it up on the street three miles from the stadium and sold it on the evil Internet for a thousand dollars."

Colin lifted a brow. "Three miles?"

"Heard tell." Mick's lips twitched.

"Uh-huh. Since when is the Internet evil?"

"Since I can't figure the blasted thing out. I mean where *is* the Internet? How does it work? What does it *do* when we aren't paying attention?"

Mick possessed the suspicious nature of a lifelong newsman. Colin had learned early on that paranoia led him to some of the best stories. Paranoia was a good trait for a journalist to have. However . . .

"Don't you use the Internet for research?" He couldn't imagine life without it.

"That's what libraries are for."

Colin glanced around the office. "You don't even have a computer."

"Don't understand them, either."

He'd fallen through the looking glass and into a parallel universe, which had captivated him.

Mick returned to his desk and lit a cigarette. The scent brought a wave of nostalgia. Whenever Colin smelled smoke, he thought of his dad, and he missed him.

"Those things will kill you," Colin was compelled to point out.

"So will a bus."

Mick leaned back and blew smoke at the ceiling. Colin grinned. That was exactly what his dad would have said — back when he'd been smoking. However, a heart attack had compelled him to do what years of nagging could not. He'd quit, but John Luchetti still missed his cigarettes.

"Your turn." Mick flicked a tail of gray

ash onto the floor.

They'd been swapping stories as they worked. The afternoon had flown by. Colin didn't want to leave, so he took a seat.

"There was this time in Israel. I was going to meet a man. Actually, he was a spy."

"For who? Us? Them? Someone else?"

"I don't know. I was coming up to a café when all of a sudden there was this flash, so bright I thought a star had hit the ground. The earth shook. I never heard the explosion. My ears just started ringing. I was on the ground and there were people running past me. The café was dust."

Mick sighed. "Think they were after him?"

"They're after anyone they can get."

"Are you always in the middle of a war, a crisis, something blowing up?"

Colin thought about it. "Pretty much."

"I'd think that would get old."

"You'd think, wouldn't you?"

But it hadn't. He loved living on the edge. Day to day, city to city, story to story. He missed it desperately. Telling his tales all afternoon had only reminded him how much he loved his job.

"You know what?" Mick took another

long draw on his cigarette, then let the smoke trail out as he spoke. "People round here have been complainin' about the ho-hum nature of my *Weekly*."

"You don't say."

Mick muttered something that sounded suspiciously like "Smart-ass" and kept talking. "Those stories you've been tellin' all day are damned good."

"Thanks."

"You wanna tell 'em to my readers?"

Colin blinked. "How?"

"In the paper, genius. Where you think? Over the loudspeaker at the Labor Day picnic?"

"There's a Labor Day picnic?"

Mick rolled his eyes. "Whaddaya say?"

Colin shrugged. He didn't have anything else to do, and he'd always liked telling stories.

"I can't pay you for those, either," Mick warned.

"Another offer I can't refuse."

"Here." The old man got to his feet. "You can use my baby." He pointed to the Smith Corona.

"Uh, I think I'll use my computer."

"Chicken?"

"No thanks, I'm not hungry."

Mick snorted. "Come on, don't be a

scaredy-cat. Write it out. The one you just told me. That'll give me time to edit before we put the thing into production."

"Edit?"

"You know — where you write something, then I fix it?"

"Maybe it won't need fixing."

"In your dreams."

Colin stared at the typewriter and his fingers itched. The last time he'd used one had been at his desk in his room on the farm. Back then he'd hated typing, hated having to white out mistakes or retype the whole damned thing.

But back then his prose had been pure. He'd had to think before he hit a key, make sure he was saying exactly what he wanted to before he said it. His stories had been tightly woven, without a single wasted word. The way newspaper articles were supposed to be.

He moved around the desk, sat in Mick's chair, his fingers poised over the keys. Moments later the typewriter went *clickety-clack,* and Colin was lost in the past.

Marlie crossed the street with a spring in her step and excitement in her heart. Soon she would see Colin.

Despite the somewhat odd and even upsetting nature of Garth's visit, she'd managed to put it behind her and enjoy the day. The children were adorable. Houdini actually stayed in his cage. She was somewhat disappointed when Colin didn't arrive for lunch, but she couldn't expect him there every day.

She let herself into the house. Her mother called a greeting from the living room, and Marlie joined her there.

Her smile faded at the sight of her mother enjoying her afternoon martini all alone. "Where's Colin?"

"Haven't seen him."

Marlie's heart started to thud faster. "Where did he go?"

"He doesn't tell me his schedule."

Because he didn't have a schedule. He had nothing to do. What if he'd left?

She hurried upstairs, but his suitcase was there and so was his computer. His car was outside. She was being silly.

But when he still hadn't arrived and dinner was over, when he still hadn't called and she was playing a haphazard game of hide-and-seek, she admitted she was worried.

For all she knew he was the kind of guy who left his belongings strewn in women's houses all over the world. Maybe she was now his Minnesota fling, and he'd be back to pick up everything some other time.

"That's enough for tonight," she announced to the children, then went inside, ignoring their groans and complaints.

"He didn't call," her mother answered, even before she asked the question — again.

Marlie drifted to the front window and stared out at the night. Her reflection disturbed her. The expression on her face was just like the one her mother wore — every time she peered outside waiting for a man who was never going to come.

With an exclamation of disgust, Marlie turned away from the glass. She was *not* going to turn into her mother. No matter what Garth said.

However, when she found herself answering the million-dollar question for Regis, she decided she had to get out of the house.

"I'm going for a walk," she said.

"Final answer," was Julie's reply.

But instead of walking, Marlie sat under the oak tree and she waited, then she waited some more. She discovered that waiting was one of the worst pastimes in the world. It gave her far too much time to think.

Maybe something terrible had happened. She should call Chief Moose.

Marlie had just gotten to her feet when footsteps thudded behind her. She spun around and nearly fainted at the sight of Colin — safe and sound — trotting across the lawn.

"Hi!" He grinned and swept her into his arms. Then he kissed her as she stood stunned. Going from fear to relief, sorrow to joy so fast made her almost as dizzy as the thoroughness of his kiss. "I missed you."

He'd missed her? He'd disappeared without a trace, a note, a call. If he'd been thinking of her enough to miss, how could that be?

"Where have you been?" she asked.

"At Mick's. I helped him all day." He was almost bouncing with excitement and reminded her of Jake after he'd won a footrace. "He gave me a job writing articles for the *Weekly*. Not that he's going to pay me, so is that really a job?" He shrugged. "I finished my first story tonight."

"Great," she said, but she couldn't quite manage any enthusiasm.

"What's the matter?" He drew back to peer at her face, then kissed her nose. "You look sad."

He truly had no idea that he'd frightened her. That she'd thought he'd slept with her, then left her behind.

"What happened, honey? Did Houdini get away for good? Did Katrina bloody someone's nose this time? Did Jake wet the mat?"

"I thought you were gone."

The words slipped out. She hadn't meant to say them. He owed her nothing. He wasn't her boyfriend, even if he was her lover.

"Gone?" he echoed. "Where?"

"Away."

"From you? Why would you think that?"

Tears taunted the corners of her eyes, and she pushed away from him so he wouldn't see her cry. She'd been foolish. He hadn't left. But that didn't make what she'd felt, what she'd believed, any less painful.

"It's nearly ten o'clock, Colin. What was I supposed to think?"

"I did something wrong." She glanced at him. His forehead creased in confusion for an instant before understanding spread across his face. "I didn't call."

"You don't have to call me. You don't owe me. That's not what I want."

"I don't owe you?"

"You think you do?" She cringed. That smacked too much of prostitution, and what she'd given him, she'd given out of love.

There. She'd admitted it, at least to herself. She loved him, and she probably always would.

He pulled her back into his arms. "I owe you for the most happiness I've felt in a long, long time."

He kissed her brow, rubbed his knuckle along her cheek. "You make me want to fly kites and play games and chase rainbows. I've never wanted to do any of those things before."

"Why not?"

She couldn't imagine a life without them.

"The world I live in is pretty dreary. The people I see are lucky to eat. They certainly don't have time to play."

"That's criminal."

"I agree. Which is why I try to change it by making people aware of what's going on."

"Is it working?"

"Not that I can see, but that doesn't mean I'm going to give up. I'm just on sabbatical."

"Which means?"

"I'm not leaving yet."

"But you will."

He took a deep breath, then let it out. "I have to."

Since she'd known that all along, Marlie wasn't surprised. He'd leave and she'd be alone again — probably forever. Now that she'd touched him, she didn't want to touch anyone else.

Marlie took his hand and led him toward the house. "Then we'd better make the most of the time we have."

CHAPTER FIFTEEN

The days passed and the nights, too. Colin fell into a routine.

He helped Mick as much as he could, mowed Marlie's lawn, played games with her mother, and at night played different ones with Marlie.

She would sneak up to his room after lights out, then sneak back down before dawn tinted the sky. That the intimate nature of their relationship was a secret, their enjoyment of each other forbidden, made every encounter more enticing.

His life wasn't so bad. Or at least that was what he kept telling himself whenever he got antsy.

He wasn't miserable. He was interested in the running of the *Weekly*. He was learning all sorts of things. He enjoyed writing stories. He was crazy about Marlie; he even liked her mom. Houdini hadn't shown up in his bed or his bath the entire time.

Life was good. *Really.*

He began to visit exotic, faraway places on the Internet late at night. With Marlie lying asleep in his bed, the moonlight turning her face marble-pale, he would stare at photos depicting the beaches of Vietnam or the ruins in Rome and he would yearn.

When he'd satisfied his craving for other places the only way he could right now, he would slip back into bed and satisfy his other craving. No matter how many times he touched her, it didn't seem to be enough.

He was torn. He wanted to go — somewhere. He needed to stay here. Though he laughed and joked and pretended he was fine, beneath the facade he was anything but.

At least Gerry came through on her promise within a few days.

"The guy's gone," she announced.

"When you say gone . . ."

"I mean *gone.* Iran doesn't have him anymore."

"Because . . . ?"

He could think of a hundred reasons, and he liked precious few of them.

"Your guess is as good as mine."

"Do you think they're lying?"

"Always. But about this . . . no. The source I have there is very good. The American they had is gone."

"Rescued, escaped, buried? What is gone?"

"I don't know. Regardless, it wasn't your brother, anyway."

Time seemed to slow. Colin's words came out sounding as if he was speaking from a deep, dark well. "How do you know that?"

"Because the guy's name was George. Sergeant George Caldwell."

Colin wasn't sure if he should be happy or not. While it was good Bobby hadn't been a prisoner, it was bad that he hadn't turned up somewhere.

Now he owed Gerry a favor. She'd probably want his firstborn, which worked out well for him since he didn't plan to have one.

That he was conducting a torrid affair with his brother's girl didn't help his state of mind. No matter how many times Marlie assured him she didn't feel anything but friendship for Bobby, Colin still felt like a traitor. Nevertheless, he couldn't give her up.

The heat wave ended as a cool, autumn wind blew through town. Colin stood at the window one night, sniffing the air, wondering where it came from, where it was going.

Marlie stirred in his bed. "Colin?"

"Right here."

She sat up, and her hair tumbled over her face. Impatiently she shoved it back, the movement pulling the bodice of her nightgown tight across her breasts. His body responded in the usual manner.

He'd already had to go to the next town to buy condoms. They'd run through all of his, and there was no way he was going to buy any in Wind Lake. He'd probably turn around and discover Victor right behind him.

"Can't sleep again?" she asked.

"No."

From across the room his computer spread artificial light. He could see the picture he'd been staring at before the wind had drawn him to the window.

The Statue of Liberty.

He wanted to see her again.

And suddenly he had an idea. A wonderful, brilliant, catastrophic idea.

He glanced at Marlie. What if when he left, he took her with him?

"I can't go to New York City." Marlie shook her head. "You're crazy."

"Why am I crazy? You've never seen New York."

266

"I've never seen the inside of a jail, either, but I know I'd rather not."

"Now you're just being stubborn."

"I like it here."

"If you've never been to New York, then how do you know you won't like it better there?"

A valid point, but she still didn't want to go.

Marlie had never been anywhere; she just wasn't interested. But suddenly Colin wanted to go to New York, and he wanted her to go with him.

He'd been restless, and every morning she awoke half expecting him to be gone. But he continued to stay, and each day she fell a little bit more deeply in love.

For that reason alone, she said, "Okay. I guess a weekend in New York won't hurt me."

Carol was back from her vacation, and Marlie arranged to have the substitute take over for her on Friday at noon. The plane left from Minneapolis around suppertime.

She told Carol and everyone else who asked that she needed to help Colin in his search for Bobby. Why that required a trip to New York, she couldn't say. Thankfully, no one asked.

Marlie hated lying, but she couldn't exactly tell people she was traipsing off to have all-night monkey sex with a man she'd only known a few weeks. Folks looked down on that in a preschool teacher.

"There's a sixties marathon on the Game Show Channel," her mother said when Marlie told her of their plans. "I won't even know you're gone."

So much for being needed.

Nevertheless, Marlie phoned Garth and asked him to stop over a few times daily. It was the first time she'd talked to him since his left-field marriage proposal.

"You're going where?" he shouted. "People disappear in New York. The place is Sin City."

"I thought that was Las Vegas."

"There can't be more than one city of sin?"

"You sound like an Old Testament prophet."

"Let's hope I'm not."

"Let's," she agreed, her voice dripping with sarcasm. Jake was enthusiastic about the idea of taking Houdini home for the weekend. Until he found out why.

"You can't go to New York. You live here."

"It's a visit. I'll be right back at Chasing Rainbows on Monday."

Jake shook his head morosely. "No, you won't."

No matter what she said to convince him, he didn't believe her.

"Grown-ups always say they'll come back, and then they don't."

Marlie had a hard time arguing with that. Her dad had done the very same thing.

Unfortunately, Jake managed to bring all the children over to his point of view so that by Friday, they were all in tears.

"Go," Carol said, pushing her toward the door.

"But —"

"What do you tell moms when their kids cry the first day?"

"They'll stop as soon as you leave."

Carol raised an eyebrow.

"Oh, all right." Marlie sighed and glanced longingly at the wailing children.

She wanted to gather them to her and promise she would never leave them. She very nearly did. Then Colin stepped into the room. He flinched at the volume of the noise. "What's going on?"

"They're afraid I'll never come back."

He shook his head. "This is what you get for never leaving." Taking her elbow, he steered her toward the door. "It'll be good for them. They shouldn't be so dependent on you."

"Are you completely heartless?"

"When I've got a plane to catch, yes." He caught a glimpse of her face and hesitated. "I'm sorry. You're really upset."

He glanced at the kids. Their cries increased in volume. He left Marlie by the door and crossed the room, then crouched in front of them. Everyone went silent.

"I'll take care of her," he promised. "Don't worry."

"Bad things happen, and there's nothin' you can do to stop 'em." Jake held Houdini in his lap as his lip pouched out belligerently. "My daddy says so."

Marlie's heart turned over. Jake's mommy dying had been a very bad thing.

"That's true. But bad things happen everywhere. If we hide in our houses, then the bad guys win."

"Bad things happen everywhere?" Victor's lip trembled. "Even in Wind Lake?"

"Nice one," Marlie muttered, and took a step toward Victor.

"Even here," Jake said. "But not as much, right?"

Marlie froze. Jake was talking to Colin, and for the first time in a long time he wasn't sneering when he did it.

"Right," Colin agreed.

Jake nodded as if he'd known that all along. "Don't be a wussy, Victor."

Victor's eyes narrowed and his fists clenched. But before he could prove he wasn't a wussy, Colin interceded. "I need Miss Marlie's help, and she needs a little break. You guys understand that, don't you?"

Victor tilted his head, and his hands relaxed as he became distracted by the new thought. "Like my mommy needs a break sometimes?"

"No doubt."

"Then how come she don't lock herself in the bathroom with a pretty bottle of grown-up grape juice? That always works for my mom. She's a whole lot happier when she's done with her break."

"I bet." Colin's voice was dry. "Miss Marlie needs a bigger break, because there's a whole lot more of you. Understand?"

Victor shrugged. "I guess."

Colin straightened and came toward her. The children had stopped crying. They even seemed to have forgotten she was leaving, since they ran off to play Duck, Duck, Goose at Carol's urging.

"Thanks," she said.

271

"No problem." He glanced over his shoulder. "They probably won't even notice you're gone."

Which was exactly what she was afraid of. If the children or her mother didn't miss her, who would? If she dropped off the face of the earth, would anyone notice? That was a sad testament to her life.

"Cappin's brother?" Jake tugged on Colin's jeans.

"Yeah?"

Marlie smiled as Colin went down on one knee. Maybe the two of them were going to be friends.

Jake whipped Houdini out from behind his back and stuck the guinea pig's nose in Colin's face. "Give us a kiss."

Or maybe not.

Six hours later, Marlie wished she'd listened to her instincts and stayed with the children.

She'd actually enjoyed flying. It was the falling she didn't care for.

They'd traveled first-class. Colin was trying to impress her and she loved him for it. From the moment they'd stepped on the plane, they'd been pampered. Champagne, hot towels, large seats, glossy magazines.

Then the pilot spoke. "Ladies and gentlemen, we are about to begin our descent into New York's LaGuardia Airport. Please take your seats."

She felt the plane shift and begin to fall.

"What's wrong?" Colin asked when he noticed her white-knuckled grip on the arms of her chair.

"F-falling," she whispered.

"No, we're making our descent. You heard the captain."

Her stomach rolled and her skin went clammy. In her head, she knew they weren't falling, but tell it to her body.

Marlie grabbed for the white paper bag and lost her first-class meal.

Colin was wonderful, getting her a cold towel this time and holding her head. By the time she stopped throwing up, they were on the ground, and then she no longer needed to.

"I'm sorry. I'm sorry."

She apologized to him, her fellow passengers, the airline attendants. Everyone was sympathetic, but she felt like a complete hick.

They waited until everyone had gotten off the plane. Then Colin collected their bags and held out his hand.

Marlie hesitated. "Maybe I should just take the return trip."

"The worst is over, honey. So you don't like flying. Big deal."

"It seems like all I do around you is throw up."

"And don't think I haven't noticed." He winked. "As long as you're around me, I'm happy."

Since that was the sweetest thing anyone had ever said to her, Marlie put her hand into his and let him show her New York.

Colin had come to New York his freshman year of college. On a train from Boston, he'd seen the skyline for the first time and he'd felt a connection.

There was always something happening. Anytime of the day or night, you could walk out on the street and never be alone.

The lights shone brighter, the music played louder, the food tasted better. He wanted to share it all with her.

"The Marriott Marquis," he told the cabdriver.

The cabbie mumbled something in another language, then took off in the direction of Manhattan.

"Does he know where he's going?" Marlie contemplated the back of the driver's turbaned head.

"Better than I do. Relax. Enjoy the

scenery." He put his arm around her shoulders and tugged her close.

Colin was in heaven. His favorite city and his favorite girl. What more could he ask?

His brother — safe and alive — but he wasn't going to worry about that. At least not this weekend.

"We'll go to the Statue of Liberty tomorrow," he said. "Ellis Island, too, if we can. Then we'll walk back and I'll show you Chinatown, Little Italy, the Village. We'll go shopping at Macy's. I'll buy you . . . anything you want."

She was staring past him out the window, her eyes wide behind her huge glasses. He followed her gaze. The city was streaming by at an alarming rate. New York cabdrivers didn't worry about little things like speed limits. They had places to go, people to deliver.

"You know what?" He shifted his head so she couldn't see out the window anymore. "It's probably best if you *don't* watch the scenery. Watch me, instead."

She gave a wan smile. "My favorite thing."

"That's my girl. On Sunday I'll take you to Tavern on the Green, then we'll walk in the park with everyone else. Would you like to go to the top of the Empire State Building?"

She paled. "Not in this lifetime."

"Are you afraid of heights?"

"No, I'm afraid of low-flying planes."

She had a point.

"Fine. No Empire State Building. Is there anyplace you'd like to visit? Ground Zero?"

She shook her head and hugged herself. He had to agree. He'd been there once and the site of the terrorist attack on the World Trade Center, even prettied up, still depressed him. He didn't think anything would ever make that scarred land right again — and maybe it shouldn't.

He searched around for something to lighten their sober mood and found it.

"Look." He pointed through the front window of the cab. "Isn't it great?"

Ahead of them the flare of neon spread toward the moon. The lights of Broadway, Fifth Avenue, Times Square all warred with each other to be the biggest and the brightest.

The cab pulled up outside the Marriott. Billboards hocked their wares up and down the avenue. Tourists and natives thronged the sidewalks together.

Colin hopped out and drew her with

him. While he paid the cabbie and gathered their overnight cases, she stared up at the colors and the lights.

"What do you think?" he asked.

She blinked, opened her mouth, then shut it again. His smile faded. She hated it.

But then she turned, kissed him on the cheek and whispered, "I think it's great."

And the lights shone brightly once more.

CHAPTER SIXTEEN

Marlie felt as if she were in hell. The noise, the smell, the garish lights, the never-ending throng of people speaking too loudly in a hundred different languages.

She'd wanted to go home from the moment she stepped off the plane, but Colin loved it here.

He led her into the hotel, all glass and marble. There were just as many people inside as out.

She glanced at her watch. It was nearly midnight! At home the entire town would be in bed. The streets peaceful, safe. God, how she missed Wind Lake.

"We're on the eleventh floor." Colin held a key card in his hand. "Not too high, but high enough to see a few things."

"Great." Marlie followed him to the elevators.

They were made of glass. She could watch as they lifted off the floor and sped toward the ceiling. What sadist had invented see-through elevators?

She turned away, but Colin kept his face

nearly pressed to the window. "Don't you love that feeling? When your stomach seems to stay down there, while your body is all the way up here?"

" 'Love' isn't exactly what I'd call it."

They were standing in front of their room and he was putting the key card into the door when it hit her. She was staying in a hotel room with a man. Now *that* was exciting. Much more so than the Statue of Liberty.

The door opened and artificially chilled air brushed her face. Colin swept out his arm. "After you, m'lady."

Marlie stepped inside. A king-size bed, a sofa, a television encased in an armoire. Their own coffeepot. What more did a person need?

She turned, and the first sight of Colin leaning against the wall hit her like a fist to the chest. She needed him.

His blue eyes sparkled with excitement. He seemed to crackle with energy. He appeared taller, broader, more confident.

She was seeing the true Colin Luchetti — in his world, a world that he loved, a world that he ruled. Despite the jeans, the suspenders, the Golden Gophers T-shirt, he belonged here.

And she did not.

That she didn't belong was never more apparent than the next day as they gallivanted about New York.

Marlie had never thought to use the word *gallivanted* in everyday life, except it fit *this* life.

Colin dragged her through several rings of hell — make that boroughs of New York. Everywhere they went was loud, hot, dirty. Everywhere they went, he said, "Isn't this great?"

Her answer was always, "Great."

Since they were in hell, she figured it was okay to lie through her teeth.

Marlie had always been a part of Wind Lake and Wind Lake a part of her. There she belonged, thrived. Here she was lost, adrift. Miserable. But she put on a happy face — for him.

They attended a Broadway play that night. How he got tickets at the last minute, she had no idea. She was stunned by the size of the place.

"I thought Broadway theaters were huge."

"If they were all huge, then there wouldn't be such a scramble for tickets. Smaller is also better for the acoustics."

What she didn't know about the world would fill an encyclopedia. She felt hopelessly inadequate, a yokel, and that was *before* the woman approached them.

During intermission Colin bought Marlie a glass of wine at the bar in the foyer. She sipped the chardonnay and contemplated all the beautiful people. The clothes were amazing. Lush fabrics, vibrant colors, styles she'd never seen put together in ways she would never have imagined.

Her best dress — an off-white, lacy confection with peach roses peppered across the skirt — was laughable under these circumstances. She was a sow's ear pretending to be a silk purse, and she had a feeling everyone knew it.

"Colin, baby, I didn't know you were in town."

Marlie had turned away to observe the crowd. She turned back and found a gorgeous, bone-thin, exquisitely dressed, perfectly made-up slut hanging all over Colin.

"Why didn't you call me?" she purred, practically drooling on his collar.

"Uh, Cleo, this is Marlie." He held out his hand to her. Marlie took a sip of her wine and ignored it.

Cleo kept her fingers on him as she let her sharp, green eyes skim Marlie. She dismissed her with a flip of her ebony hair. "You're kidding me, right?"

Colin disengaged himself from the woman's grasping fingers and slid his hand around Marlie's waist. "It was nice seeing you, Cleo, but if you'll excuse us, the play is about to start again."

"Is she your cousin or something?" The horrible woman followed them toward the door. "You can't be screwing her. I mean, really, Colin, have you no standards?"

He stiffened. "Cleo, knock it off. Your claws are showing."

Cleo gasped. "I don't hear from you for months, then you have the nerve to show your face with that . . . that . . ."

People were starting to stare. Marlie's face heated. Colin pulled her with him through the crowd and back toward their seats.

Cleo shouted after them. "I won't even discuss the prom dress, but what about those glasses? Did you find them at a dime store?"

They reached their seats just as the lights went down. Marlie discovered she was much more comfortable in the dark.

"Honey, I'm sorry. She's a little nuts."

"Obviously she was *your* little nut at one time."

"Not really."

"She seems to think so."

He shook his head. "Let's talk about this later."

"Fine."

Marlie returned her attention to the play, but the night was ruined. Not that it had been all that great to begin with. She wanted to go home.

Colin took her to his favorite restaurant, where everyone knew him.

Everyone knew Marlie at her favorite restaurant, too, but then, there was only one in the whole darn town. She liked it that way.

They sat at a secluded booth in the back. He bought her champagne.

She took a sip and the bubbles shot straight up her nose. Choking, she coughed, and the champagne flew out of both nostrils. Wasn't that attractive?

Marlie set the glass down and sighed. "Colin, take me home."

In the middle of reaching for her, he paused, hand still in the air. "What? Why?"

"I don't fit in here."

"Don't listen to Cleo. She's like that because she never eats. It'd make anyone cranky."

"Look at me." Marlie waved her hands

in a circular motion to indicate her dress, her glasses . . . her.

"I'm always looking at you. I can't stop. You're beautiful."

She snorted. Big mistake. Her nose still hurt from the champagne enema.

He threw up his hands. "I'll buy you a new dress. Contacts, too. Will that help?"

"No."

"Why not?"

"I don't want a new dress and I don't want contacts."

She liked her glasses. She could hide behind them.

"What *do* you want?"

"I want to go home. With you."

"I've got no home. You know that."

"You could have." She swallowed, then plunged ahead. "With me."

He stared at her for a long time as his elegant, piano-man fingers played with the stem of his glass. She wished she could read his face, but everything he felt was kept hidden behind his somber eyes.

"Why don't we go to the hotel?" he murmured.

"Why don't we?"

They were silent on the walk back. Colin wasn't sure what to say or what to do. He'd showed her his world, and she hated it. Almost as much as he hated hers.

He let them into their room. The place was sparkling, pristine. He loved hotel rooms. You messed them up, then left, and when you came back, everything was clean and new again.

Colin glanced at Marlie. The sadness on a face that was genetically happy disturbed him. Like a wildflower taken out of the field and left on the side of the road, she was wilting here. He had to take her back before everything that was special about her was gone.

Pulling her into his arms, he buried his face in her hair. She still smelled like honey and vanilla, scents of home and hearth, scents that would forever remind him of her.

She clung to him, hands roaming, fingers seeking. Her nails scraped across his belly as she yanked his fresh new shirt from his brand-new slacks. A quick trip to Macy's had allowed him to throw the Wind Lake jeans and Golden Gopher T-shirt into the trash.

"We should talk," he murmured as his lips traced her temple, then her cheek.

"Not now."

Winding her fingers around the back of

his neck, she drew his mouth to hers, kissing him with a wild desperation.

This was goodbye, and he wasn't ready.

He tried to pull back, to calm her with gentle kisses across her eyes, her forehead, but she would have none of it.

She'd already unbuttoned his shirt, loosened his tie and gone for his zipper. Her lips trailed across his chest; her palm cupped him. Her hand closed around him, and he was lost. If this was goodbye, he'd make it one that both of them would remember.

Forever.

They tumbled onto the perfectly made bed. Somehow his shirt ended up tangled at his wrists, his tie trailing down his bare chest.

Marlie straddled him, trailing the edge of the silk tie across his stomach. His muscles shuddered and contracted; she tugged on the knot, pulling him up until their lips met.

With his hands caught and his body pinned, he was at her mercy. He didn't mind.

Her tongue ran along the seam of his lips, then delved inside and danced with his. Her hands perched on his shoulders, her fingers kneaded the muscles, then dropped down to tease his nipples.

He groaned and struggled until his wrists popped free of his shirt as the cloth ripped. His palms cupped her hips and urged her closer. She scooted in, pressing herself against his erection. Her sharp gasp of shock and arousal lifted her breasts in an enticing dance.

He fumbled with the zipper of her dress, got it stuck and nearly cursed with frustration. But the gods took pity on him, and with his second try, the thing slid open.

She tugged the garment over her head and tossed it away. Beneath the cream-colored dress, she wore a lacy black slip. A fashion faux pas, no doubt, but he didn't mind. The dark silk made her skin glow like alabaster in the light from the lamp on the desk.

He ran his palms up her smooth, pantyhosecovered thighs. The waistband had cut a red welt, which he kissed and touched gently as he removed the offending hose.

Beneath the slip she wore plain white underwear and a sturdy matching bra. She lay on the bed, the slip shoved to her waist, the virginal nature of her undergarments a stark contrast to the wild, tangled length of her hair. Just looking at her made him pulse hard and hot. If he wasn't careful, this would be over before they even got started.

He discarded his clothes and, running his fingers up her thigh, reveled in the quivering muscles beneath her skin. So fine, so strong, so much a part of her.

He urged her out of the slip. Though he was sorry to see it go, he needed to feel all that soft, milky skin against his.

Releasing the clasp of her bra, her beautiful breasts sprang free. He buried his face in the smooth flesh. Everything about her was round, pale, exquisite. She was perfect, and for now she was his.

Her arms closed around him as she whispered his name. His body seemed to leap forward of its own accord. He had to be inside her. He couldn't think of anything else.

With one firm stroke he was there. Warm and tight, she held him in an intimate embrace. He paused, afraid if he moved at all, he'd come right then. She stroked his hair, ran her fingertips down his back, and then she began to move against him.

"Honey, wait . . ."

There was something he needed to do, but he couldn't quite recall what. Then any thoughts were burned to cinders as his body ignited and his mind went up in flames.

He couldn't be still any longer. He followed her lead, sliding in to the hilt, then out to the tip. He could feel her quivering on the edge, enticing him to go there with her. She took him ever deeper, and as she clenched around him, she whispered, "I love you. I will *always* love you."

The words that should have sent him running, should have cooled his ardor into ice-cold dread, instead made him come hard and fast, two becoming one, in the way this was meant to be.

He leaned his forehead against hers. It didn't matter who she was, who he was, what his brother felt or didn't. The truth was in his heart, and he could no longer deny it.

Colin lifted his head and stared into Marlie's eyes. "I love you, too."

Her smile was worth a thousand days in purgatory, which was no doubt where he was headed at the instant of his death. But he wasn't going to worry about that when his life seemed to have just begun.

She cupped his cheek, lifted her mouth, brushed her lips across his. Their breaths mingled, their bodies still joined. He wanted to stay like this forever.

How quickly things change.

With a blinding burst of clarity, Colin remembered what he'd forgotten, and suddenly death didn't look half-bad.

"Condom," Colin muttered, and leaped out of bed.

Marlie, still warm and fuzzy from the sex and the declaration of love, lay there dazed and dopey.

At first, what he'd said did not compute. When it did, the warmth was a memory and a chill wind seemed to sweep the room.

He'd forgotten to use a condom, and from the expression on his face, that was a sin for which there was no absolution. She wasn't saying she was thrilled, but she didn't want to throw up in the garbage can for a change. Colin appeared as if he just might.

"Dammit," he said harshly.

She winced. What had happened to the man who had sweetly whispered, "I love you, too," while still buried deep inside her?

Had that only been a few moments ago? She'd had plenty of time to build a dream.

Home, marriage, family. Sweet babies with her eyes and his hair.

She sat up and wrapped the bedspread around her.

Standing, she tried to walk away. But the bedspread stuck where it seemed to have been glued between the mattresses. With an irritated yank, she freed the thing. "I *hate* hotels," she muttered. "They always have to *fix* everything."

Why was she talking about hotels when there were more upsetting matters at hand? Namely, she could be pregnant right this minute.

Joy filled her, so strong and pure she was dazzled. Her eyes teared up, and she turned her back so he wouldn't see, but Colin saw everything.

He put his hands on her shoulders and drew her back against his chest. "I'm sorry. I'm so sorry, honey. It's my fault. I couldn't think. I just . . ." His hands clenched and his lips brushed her hair. "I needed to be with you. I had to . . . touch you. I loved you. I mean, I *love* you."

"And for that you're sorry," she whispered.

"No. Of course not. I'm sorry about losing my head. I've never done that before."

"Well, what a relief."

"I'll make everything all right. I promise."

How did he plan on doing that when she no longer knew what right was?

"Don't cry, Marlie. It isn't the end of the world."

He sounded as if he was trying to convince himself of that. She turned in his arms. "You think I'm crying because . . . ?"

"I might have gotten you pregnant." He pulled at his hair as if he'd like to yank it out. "God, I'm *sorry.*"

Her stomach rolled in a sickening wave as a horrible thought took root in her mind.

"You don't want children, do you."

"Of course not." His mouth turned down as if he'd smelled something foul. "The world is screwed up enough."

His words were like a punch to her gut.

"And a baby would screw it up more?"

"There are more children in this world than we need."

Marlie tugged the bedspread more tightly around her neck as the cold seeped in. "How could we ever have more than we need of something so wonderful?"

He cast her a quick glance. "Marlie, you live in a gilded world where children are sweet and cute. They all have enough to eat, clean clothes and people who love them."

"For the most part."

"But the rest of the world, the real world, isn't like that."

"You think I don't live in the real world?"

"Wind Lake is a little piece of . . ."

"What?"

"Heaven for you, I guess. Like Jake said, bad things happen a lot less there."

"So?"

"If you'd seen what I've seen, been where I've been, you'd agree with me. Bringing more children into this mess of a world is a very bad idea."

"Even if you'll love them with all your heart?"

His shoulders sagged on a long sigh. "You want kids. I guess I should have suspected that."

"What would have been your first clue?" Her mouth was getting out of hand. But from what she'd seen of New York, no one would care. They wouldn't even notice.

"You're good with them. I'm not. Kids make me nervous. I want to be anywhere but near them. And babies . . ." He shuddered. "They give me the creeps. All that crying. What do they want?"

"It's a mystery."

"I lived in a house with too many children. I decided a long time ago that I didn't want any. I should have told you, but . . . when exactly is the appropriate time to bring something like that up?"

Before she fell in love with him would have been ideal, Marlie thought, but this time she kept the words to herself.

Though she felt as if her entire world was crumbling around her, Marlie herself didn't crumble. "What did you mean when you said you loved me?"

He appeared confused again. "Just that."

"*Just* that. I see."

And she did. He'd meant love as he knew it. Companionship, fun, sex. A slightly deeper emotion than he'd felt for anyone else who'd flitted through his life up until now. *Just* that.

But to her, love meant forever.

"I'm going to get dressed." She headed for the bathroom. He caught her before she took three steps.

"No. Wait. You *don't* see. I love you. I want to make a life with you."

Hope, that evil beast, flickered to life. Marlie was, above all things, an optimist.

"Really?"

He held her close and kissed her. She tasted a promise on his lips, and she melted into him.

"Really," he murmured against her neck. His hand slipped beneath the bedspread and his palm laid claim to her waist. "We'll get you a passport, hire someone to take over the day care. They can live with your mom, too. It'll be terrific, Marlie. I'll show you the world."

The little flicker of hope died with a near-audible *poof*.

"I can't leave the children or my mother."

"They'll be well taken care of. I promise. I need you with me."

"I need you with me. In Wind Lake."

Pure revulsion crossed his face. "I can't stay there. I've got to travel, investigate, write."

"And I have to nest, care for and cuddle."

"Take care of *me*."

She was tempted. Oh, how she was tempted. She'd been dreaming the dream for so long — love, home, family — never thinking she'd have any of them. Now she'd found love, and it was as wonderful as she'd dreamed it would be.

But what happened when your dream was another person's nightmare?

There was a song . . . Something about two out of three ain't bad. What did they say about one out of three?

Marlie knew what she had to say. "I'm sorry, Colin, but I need more than that."

CHAPTER SEVENTEEN

Colin was still stunned the next morning as they caught a cab to the airport.

Marlie had called the airline last night while still wearing the bedspread and gotten them on a plane back to Minneapolis in the morning. He was too out of it to argue.

They'd slept in the same bed, but they might as well have been in different time zones. She clung to the edge on her side. He kept to the left of the imaginary line.

How had everything gone wrong so fast? She was behaving as if it was over. But he loved her and she loved him. They could work this out. Somehow. He just wasn't sure how.

His cell phone rang as they reached the gate. Marlie took his bag, then took a seat. Colin moved into a quiet corner and answered the phone.

"Colin, get your tail to Pakistan."

Colin nearly hung up. He might owe his boss a favor, but he wasn't going to Pakistan while Marlie's eyes were so sad.

"I just got a call from one of my contacts. Your brother walked into a hospital in Peshawar."

His heart gave a hard, painful thud and then began to race. "Is he hurt?"

"I don't know."

"I'm on my way."

Colin flipped his phone shut and let his gaze stray to Marlie. The sight of her made his chest tighten. He loved her so much. He didn't want to go until they worked things out, but the only thing that could make him leave her had happened.

His brother was alive.

She glanced up. Their gazes met and she frowned. He crossed the short distance separating them.

"What is it?" she asked.

"Bobby showed up at a hospital in Pakistan."

Joy spread over her face. His gut clenched.

"You're so beautiful." The words slipped out. He couldn't stop them.

She snorted. "And you're so blind. Tell me about Bobby."

He opened his mouth to argue and the loudspeaker announced the boarding of their flight.

She stood. "That's us. You'd better tell me on the plane."

"I've got to go."

"We both do." She nodded toward the gate.

"To Pakistan."

"Why?"

"They won't give us any information. We don't know if he's hurt. I'm the only one familiar with the area."

She studied him, then gave a half laugh. "You can't wait to leave."

He blinked. "What?"

"I can see it in your eyes, on your face. The thought of traipsing off to Whatsistan excites you."

"I'm happy my brother is alive. I want to see him. Of course I'm excited."

"And it's an added bonus that he's turned up in the Middle East, rather than Wind Lake."

The loudspeaker crackled, "Last call for Minneapolis."

Marlie glanced at the gate. "I need to go."

"You could come with me."

"Even if I did have a sudden urge to travel to a place where Americans are viewed as scum, I don't have a passport."

Damn.

He hesitated. "Maybe I should go back with you. Catch a plane from there."

"To Pakistan? I don't think so. Besides, you need to get over there. Why waste time?" She patted his arm as if he were one of her kids. "Let me know how he is, okay?"

He grabbed her hand before she could scoot away. "You act like you'll never see me again."

"Will I?"

"Of course. I'll call you as soon as I talk to him. And when I get back . . ." He trailed off, uncertain where to go with that.

"Right." Her smile was both sweet and sad. "There's no place for me in your world and no world for you in my place." She went up on tiptoe and brushed his lips with hers. "Thank you for everything."

He was so shocked he barely responded to the kiss. She was blowing him off like last week's lint.

"Everything?" he repeated numbly.

"I'll always be grateful for the time we had and what we shared."

She walked away. He felt like a gigolo.

"I'll be back," he called after her. "I promise."

She disappeared down the gangplank without so much as a glance or a wave. He watched until the plane was a little dot in the bright blue sky, and then he made his way to the international terminal.

When he got off the plane in Peshawar, he still missed her so much his stomach hurt. Would the pain ever go away? Colin didn't think so.

He meant to call her. Really he did. Except when he arrived at the hospital, his brother was gone.

"Gone?" he shouted at the harried doctor. "Gone where?"

"I do not know."

Since most educated Pakistanis spoke English, the official language of the country, Colin had little trouble questioning the man.

"Was he hurt?"

"Not that I could see."

"Then why was he in this hospital?"

"He brought us an injured child from the streets."

"Where is this child?"

The doctor's face clouded. "Sadly, the child did not survive."

"And my brother?"

"He was here, and then he was not."

"Did the army come for him?"

"Not that I am aware of."

The doctor rushed off. Colin kicked the wall and cursed. Everyone in the vicinity inched away.

He made a few phone calls, didn't find out one damn thing. The army knew nothing — or if they did they weren't saying. Big surprise.

After leaving a message for his mother, he started to call Marlie. Just as he was dialing her number, a young Pakistani man sidled up to him.

"You are looking for the American captain?"

"Yes."

Once again, the conversation was in English, which was lucky because Colin's Punjabi, the most widely spoken language in Pakistan, was pretty bad.

"I can show you which way he went."

"He left on his own?"

The young man beckoned. "This way."

Colin had known better than to go off with a stranger since he was three, but he did it anyway.

The kid led him down one street and up another, through an alley to a run-down house. Colin studied the place. Was Bobby still here? And if so, why? Only one way to find out.

He walked to the door and knocked. A shuffle was his only warning before something hit him hard from behind, and the world went black.

Colin awoke to pounding pain beneath his eyes. He opened them, and for a moment he believed he was blind. Then he realized the darkness was so complete he could barely see his hand in front of his face.

Water dripped somewhere close by. He lay on damp, rough stones, and he ached all over. He must have been here a long time.

When he tried to get up, agony flared even more sharply than before. Suddenly he remembered what had happened. The kid, the house, the smack on the head. He was in trouble.

Nausea swirled in his belly, both from the thought of his family hearing he'd been kidnapped and from the intense pain. But what really made him sick was Marlie. He'd promised her he'd come back. What was she going to think when he didn't?

That he'd had his fun and left her behind. Colin groaned. Worse, what if word of his abduction was spread all over CNN? She'd hear it and be terrified.

This was what he got for wanting to be famous, for wanting everyone to remember which Luchetti brother he was. Now they'd never forget. He wished he could go back to being confused with Evan.

A shuffle to his right made Colin turn his head in that direction. Something furry scrambled over his chest. He swallowed the scream. It would be better if they didn't know he was awake. Whoever *they* were.

I'll pretend that was Houdini, he told himself. If the worst thing in this room with him was a guinea pig, he'd be fine. He could handle that.

Another shuffle, this time to his left, preceded a shaft of light spilling into the room. Two men stood silhouetted in the doorway.

"Mr. Luchetti," one said in the melodic accent of Pakistan. "We have some questions for you."

Colin closed his eyes. He had a feeling there were worse things than rats in his cell. A lot worse.

Life went on as always in Wind Lake, one of the reasons Marlie loved the place.

Same job, same house, same people, same schedule — day in and day out. The only thing that changed were the categories on *Jeopardy!* It was comforting.

Especially when day after day, week after week passed without a word from Colin.

Why was she surprised?

One thing that *had* changed was her relationship with her best friend. Garth was still waiting for her answer to his proposal, and she was still pretending he'd never asked, which made for some awkward moments.

But if she wouldn't consider a relationship that didn't include children, how could she consider one that didn't include true love?

Life really sucked sometimes.

All her feelings for Colin were still inside her, but without him there, the emotions became pent-up. Sometimes she felt as if she might explode if she didn't see him soon.

Was this what her mother had felt for her father? If so, Marlie could understand why game shows were preferable to remembering he was gone and that she might never feel such things again.

Every morning the first thought in Marlie's head was that she faced another day without him — and that first thought made her sick. In keeping with her general behavior in relation to Colin Luchetti, she'd had to do some serious mind-over-matter concentrating to keep from upchucking to greet every sunrise. She put on a happy face, but she was miserable.

Which was her only excuse for not seeing the signs. Pathetically, her mother saw them first.

"Marlie, is there something you want to tell me?"

"Mmm?"

Engrossed in *Wheel of Fortune*, which had become Marlie's favorite show, she wasn't paying attention.

"F-L-O," she muttered. "A place. Oh! Florence. You owe me a quarter." Marlie took a sip of her iced tea.

"You're going to have a baby, aren't you?"

Marlie sprayed tea all over the floor.

Her mother gasped. "Marlie Inger Anderson! That was uncalled for."

"What did you expect me to do when you say something like that? You're lucky I didn't have a stroke."

"You'd have a stroke over the truth?"

"Mom, where do you get this stuff?"

Her mother grabbed the remote and shut Pat and Vanna off in midpuzzle. Marlie couldn't remember her mother *ever* doing something that drastic.

"I'm not blind, and contrary to your belief, I'm neither stupid or senile."

"Mom —"

"When was your last period?"

"None of your business!"

"Weight gain?"

"No. In fact, I've lost weight. I haven't been very hungry lately."

"Nausea in the morning?"

Uh-oh.

Her mother continued to list symptoms. Marlie had experienced every one. Julie clapped her hands and smiled. "A grandchild. Just what I always wanted. Your father will be so pleased."

Marlie rubbed her forehead. Wasn't this just swell?

Her mother, being her mother, never even asked who the daddy was. She just set about knitting booties during every commercial.

A visit to the doctor confirmed what Marlie already knew. She was having Colin's baby.

What was she going to do?

She stewed for a few days. Colin hadn't contacted her, even though he'd promised to. He'd made it very clear he wanted no children. Did she owe him anything?

Yes.

Though she'd rather spend a month in New York, she had to tell Colin he was going to be a father.

Marlie waited until Friday night, when

her mother was absorbed in a twenty-four-hour *Match Game* marathon, then she sneaked into her bedroom and dialed information for Gainsville, Illinois. Moments later the phone was picked up at the Luchetti farm.

"Yeah?"

"Um, hello. This must be Dean."

"Got it in one. And who must you be?"

"Marlie Anderson."

"Bobby's pen pal?"

"Yes," she said shortly. She'd called in hopes of finding Colin and she was impatient to do so. "Is Colin there?"

Silence met her question.

"Hello?"

"You don't know?"

"Know what?" she asked, but icy-cold dread already tripped down her spine.

"Colin disappeared in Pakistan over a month ago."

Marlie blinked. "But . . . but . . . I haven't seen anything on the news."

"Amazing how quiet the government can keep something if they want to, isn't it?"

"The government? I don't understand."

"All we know is that we're supposed to keep the disappearance secret. For Colin's sake."

"And Bobby? Is he home now?"

"No. He was already gone when Colin got there."

Marlie sat down heavily on her bed. She was still dizzy, so she put her head between her knees, though she kept the phone next to her ear.

"What do the authorities say?"

"Nothing worth listening to."

"Do they think he's alive?" she whispered.

"They won't say."

"Can you . . . will you let me know if you hear something?"

"I guess." He sounded confused. "Maybe you should talk to my mom. Mom!"

At his shout, what sounded like a dozen dogs began to bark so loudly on his end she could hear nothing else. Marlie hung up. She was too weak to hold the phone any longer, and she wasn't up to talking to Eleanor Luchetti. Eventually she would have to, but not today.

He'd promised to come back, just like her father always had. And like her father, he'd made a promise he couldn't keep.

The next morning she couldn't get out of bed. Nor the morning after that. Her mom was worried. She threatened to call the doctor. Marlie slammed the bedroom door in her face.

Julie brought in the big guns.

Garth walked into Marlie's room just after noon on Sunday. Marlie groaned and pulled the covers over her head. He yanked them right back off.

"You've got everyone worried, don't ya know? Tell me what's the matter."

His concern touched her. Garth cared about her, just as she cared about him. Always had, always would. Nothing could change that, so she told him everything.

"You don't know that he's dead," Garth said when she was through.

"Even if he isn't —" and she prayed every waking moment that he wasn't "— I don't know if I can live the rest of my life the way I've been living the past few days. Whenever he's not with me, I'll be worrying if he's alive, if he's hurt, dead, or ever coming back."

"Maybe once he knows about the baby, he'll want to stay here with you."

"No. He doesn't want children. Ever."

Garth blinked. "How could someone not want children? They're so —" he spread his big, gentle hands "— neat."

"I agree. Unfortunately Colin doesn't."

"Then he should have kept it in his pants," Garth muttered.

310

"This is as much my fault as his."

"I doubt it."

She smiled. Garth was such a good guy, such a great friend. The best.

Marlie took his hand. "Thanks for rushing right over. I needed my pal."

His fingers tightened on hers. "I could be more than your pal, Marlie. Maybe you should think some more about what I asked you before you went to New York."

"You still want to marry me?"

"Of course. Nothing's changed."

"If you think that, then you weren't listening."

"Nothing's changed in the way I feel about you. About us. About what I want for Jake."

"Everything would be so complicated, Garth."

"It doesn't have to be. We'll have yours, mine and hopefully, someday, ours. Remember that movie?"

"I do. Those people loved each other."

"Peanut, I love you."

"As a friend."

"Which is the best kind of love." His face clouded. "It doesn't destroy you."

Marlie frowned. Garth was avoiding life rather than living it. She didn't believe friendship was better than true love. She

311

couldn't now that she'd experienced the latter. But she also knew that sometimes love wasn't enough.

"Garth, I don't —"

"Think about the future. Your business. The life your child will have in Wind Lake."

"What's that supposed to mean?"

"It might be the twenty-first century everywhere else, but in Wind Lake it might as well be the nineteenth. You believe parents are going to want to bring their children to a preschool run by an unwed mother?"

She opened her mouth, but he kept right on talking.

"And what about the child? You don't think his lack of a father will come up in daily conversation? The word *bastard* still hurts."

Bastard? Did people actually use that term in its proper context anymore? She didn't want her child to be the one to find out.

Garth might have a point. She'd curbed her tongue, watched her step for years so that Chasing Rainbows would flourish. She couldn't say for certain that her burgeoning belly wouldn't put an end to her livelihood. Then what would she do? She had her mother to worry about, as well as the baby and herself.

"You know I'm right," Garth murmured.

She raised her gaze to his. "It wouldn't be fair to marry you to make things easier for me."

"It would make things easier for me, too. Jake preys on my mind. He needs you."

"But what if you meet someone someday you truly love, and here you are married to your best friend?"

He got up and crossed to the window, stared out, but he didn't seem to see. "I wake up in the night and I reach for her. I know she's gone, but in my dreams she's still right here."

Marlie's throat went thick, and she swallowed against the well of tears.

He turned and the stark misery on his face jolted her. "I won't meet anyone, Marlie. I believe there's someone for everyone, and Annika was for me."

"But —"

"No buts. I won't *ever* fall in love again. I can't bear to."

Silence descended between them, broken only by the canned laughter and false applause from whatever game show her mother was obsessed with that day.

After several moments, Garth murmured, "Well?"

"I have to think about this."

"Fine." He paused at the door. "But you're going to start showing soon."

"Even if I married you tomorrow, I'd start showing soon. The months aren't going to add up to nine no matter what kind of math we use. Everyone's going to know."

"Maybe. But once you're my wife, they won't say a word."

Marlie looked all the way up Garth's tree-trunk body. He was right. No one would dare. There was comfort in that.

Marlie hadn't realized how much she needed comfort until it was there. Garth and Jake hung around a lot. They ate supper at her house. Jake played games with her mother. Garth fixed the sink. It was the life she'd always dreamed of, so why wasn't she happy?

Because she didn't believe Colin was dead.

If the father of her child was dead, shouldn't she feel it? Shouldn't a part of her be an open, bleeding wound? Garth still had one. So did her mother.

Perhaps she felt this way because there'd been no closure. Wasn't that why people had funerals, for closure?

Well, she hadn't had any, so she continued to believe Colin was alive, and if he was alive, she couldn't marry Garth. Not while there was a tiny ray of hope that her entire dream could come true.

They'd questioned him for hours. What was he doing in Pakistan? Where was his brother? What was Bobby up to?

Colin only had an answer to their first question. Unfortunately, they didn't believe him.

He wasn't sure if he should be happy or terrified that they took great pains to leave no marks on his face. Did that mean they were going to photograph him dead or alive?

By the end of the first session, he really didn't care.

They left him where they'd found him — on the floor of the small, damp cell. The darkness returned. So did the rats. He continued to pretend they were Houdini. Sometimes it even worked.

He drifted on a dream. Back to Wind Lake, back to her. There he enjoyed cool autumn breezes, the laughter of children, the scent of vanilla and the touch of a woman who loved him.

The men who'd kidnapped Colin seemed to think that Bobby was involved in a mission that had to do with them. Obviously terrorists, he wasn't sure which particular faction of crazies they were associated with. They weren't scared of him; however, they did appear to be scared of Bobby.

What was his brother up to?

The army denied knowing where Bobby was, but the terrorists believed he was here somewhere. Did that mean Bobby had gone rogue — or had he just gone deeply undercover?

No one was going to tell him. Probably not even Bobby. If he ever saw his brother again.

Time passed. Colin wasn't sure if he'd been in the cell for hours or days. Maybe it was weeks.

Why had he ever wanted to leave Wind Lake? Now all he wanted was to go back. Why had he feared commitment, small towns, boredom or the threat of being average? Average men did not get kidnapped by Pakistani terrorists.

Daily they questioned him. Daily he gave them the same answers, with the same results. That they hadn't killed him yet gave him some hope. He clung to the illusion because he didn't have anything else.

Except his memories. When things got

really bad, he went to Wind Lake, flew a kite, played hide-and-seek, got his ass whupped in *Jeopardy!* and made love to Marlie beneath the light of the moon.

Thank God he had those memories. If not, he didn't know how he would have survived.

Since he only saw the inside of his dark cell, days and nights blended together. Therefore, he had no idea if it was day or night when the door opened.

A man stood in silhouette — a different man from any of those who'd come here before.

Colin's heart lurched. That couldn't be good.

"You look like shit."

Or maybe it was, because the voice was Bobby's.

CHAPTER EIGHTEEN

Bobby shut the door, flicked on a penlight and crossed the room toward Colin. He was dressed like a terrorist, looked like one, too. No wonder Colin hadn't recognized him.

"Well, if it isn't GI Joe." Colin struggled to sit up. "What the hell are you doing here?"

"I was going to ask you the same thing."

"Wasn't my idea," he muttered.

Bobby grunted and hauled him to his feet. "We're getting out of this hole."

"How did you know where to find me?"

Bobby didn't answer. Colin wasn't surprised. His brother was involved in something big, something nasty, something that had the terrorists scared out of the few wits they had.

"God, it's good to see you," Colin blurted.

"I bet."

In the small amount of light available, Bobby's grin flashed. Except for the robes, the turban and the beard, he seemed the same. Big, strong, confident. Yep, he was up to something.

"Wait a minute." Colin took his brother's chin and tilted it toward the light. "What happened to your eyes?"

All the Luchetti brothers had blue eyes. Bobby's were now brown.

"Contacts." He shrugged. "I can't very well slip around unnoticed in this country with blue eyes."

"Good point."

"Let's go. The sleepy juice I gave your pals isn't going to last forever."

He opened the door, looked both ways, then motioned for Colin to follow. As his brother crept down the hall, Bobby's robes shifted and Colin caught a glimpse of an AK-47 — the weapon of choice for terrorists.

Colin hadn't been out of his cell since he'd gone in. He had no idea where he was. The building they traversed appeared to be a warehouse of some kind.

In very little time at all, Bobby opened a door and they stepped into the night. Colin took a huge breath of air. The sky was clear; stars sparkled like diamonds against blue velvet.

He glanced around. The house where the young man had taken him was right next door. He'd been three feet from where he'd disappeared all along.

"Come on." Bobby took off at a fast clip in the direction of the hospital. Colin did his best to keep up, but he hadn't been doing very much walking lately.

Bobby turned, frowned at the way Colin was limping and threw him over his shoulder.

"Hey! Put me down."

"Sorry. I don't have time for this. I've gotta dump you at the hospital and get back to work. Call the American consulate. They'll help you."

It was difficult to talk while being carried double-time through the streets of Peshawar on someone's shoulder. But Colin had a feeling Bobby was going to disappear again soon, so he asked questions while he could.

"What are you into, bro?"

Bobby didn't answer.

"Mom's hysterical. Dad, too, though you couldn't tell by talking to him. Even Dean's worried."

Bobby snorted and Colin had to smile. Dean never worried about anyone, not even himself.

"Tell them I'm fine. And you, quit searching for me. You nearly screwed up what it took me months to build."

"Which is?"

Bobby stopped and dumped Colin unceremoniously on his feet. "None of your damn business."

Electric lights shone across the street. They were already at the hospital.

"I gotta go." Bobby's eyes, which were so foreign and strange, shifted to the shadows. The tension in him was almost palpable.

"Your superior told us you disappeared."

"I did." Bobby continued to stare into the alleyways.

"He doesn't know what you're doing, either?"

"No."

"What *are* you doing?"

Bobby turned his attention back to Colin. "I can't say and you know it."

Colin sighed. "Yeah. I do."

"Listen, they've kept your kidnapping pretty quiet. It hasn't been on the news."

"Damned near a miracle."

"I'd appreciate it if you kept as much of what happened here to yourself as you can. Okay?"

Colin nodded.

"Go home. I can't do what I have to if I'm worrying about my brother being used against me." Bobby clapped Colin on the shoulder and walked away.

"What about Marlie?"

His brother froze. "What about her? Is she all right?"

"Of course. But why did you send me to Wind Lake?"

"I got worried. I shouldn't have written to her but I was . . ." He sighed and stared up at the night. "I was lonely. Then I started thinking that maybe it wasn't such a hot idea in my situation, sending letters to a woman."

"You're saying she's in danger?" Colin's voice echoed off the stone walls.

Bobby winced. "Doubtful. I panicked. Wrote that note. I figured you'd take care of her if I couldn't."

Colin had taken care of her all right. "Would it have hurt you to be a little more explicit about what you wanted me to do?"

"Oops?"

Typical Bobby — act first, worry about consequences later. Were they brothers? Yes.

Though Bobby's actions had been a little extreme, Colin couldn't get mad about it. If Bobby hadn't overreacted, he'd never have met Marlie.

And on the bright side — Bobby wasn't crazy in love with her.

"Take care of her, man."

The words seemed to come out of thin air.

"What the hell?"

Colin ran to the last place he'd seen his brother, but Bobby had disappeared.

"I really *hate* it when you do that," Colin murmured to the empty street.

Another month passed. Marlie would have to make a decision soon.

The phone rang bright and early one Saturday morning. Her mother was still sleeping. Marlie was drinking tea and reading a book.

She glanced at her watch — seven o'clock. Who on earth would call this early on a Saturday?

Her heart clutched and she dived for the phone. "Hello?"

"Marlie?"

Her heart seemed to fall to her toes. A woman's voice.

"Yes."

"This is Eleanor Luchetti."

Marlie's heart bounced right back into her throat. "Is he . . . ?"

"Alive and well. Or at least as well as you get in a hospital in Pakistan."

"He's hurt?"

"Dehydration. Malnutrition. A few

323

bruises he shouldn't have, but he'll be all right."

Marlie sent up a little thank-you prayer. "What happened?"

"He was taken prisoner, like that poor reporter who was . . ." Eleanor's voice broke. "But he's fine. Bobby helped him get out. And those bastards . . . well, they should know better than to mess with a Luchetti."

"Bobby? He's all right?"

Eleanor's sigh hitched in the middle with suppressed tears. "He disappeared again."

"I'm sorry."

"Me, too. But at least Colin's okay, and I wanted to let you know. Dean said you were concerned. I appreciate that."

Marlie hesitated. Should she tell Colin's mother about the baby? It just didn't seem right to tell her before she told him, and it definitely didn't seem right to say something so life-changing over the phone.

"When will he be back?"

"Soon. Maybe tomorrow."

"They're releasing him already?"

"He's been in the hospital for two weeks. He's okay now."

Tears sparked Marlie's eyelids. Two weeks? And she hadn't heard a word.

She took a deep breath. "Thank you for

letting me know, Mrs. Luchetti."

Marlie hung up. Then she sat in the kitchen as her tea grew cold, and her heart settled back where it belonged.

She had to be practical. She had to think like a mother. Her baby was depending on her.

True love was a wonderful dream. But chasing rainbows was for people who could afford to. Marlie was no longer one of them.

She picked up the phone and dialed a familiar number. When it was answered, she said, "I'll marry you, Garth, just as soon as we can arrange it."

Colin turned his rented pickup truck into the long driveway that led to the Luchetti family farm. Though he'd wanted nothing more than to take a direct flight to Minneapolis, he'd been guilted into coming here first.

He couldn't really blame his mom. She'd spent weeks thinking she'd lost two sons, instead of one. When she'd begged him to come home, just for a day or two, so she could see him, touch him, how could he say no?

The American consulate had been a big help in getting him back to the States and in keeping quiet what had happened to him. Bobby was involved in something huge if he could make the kidnapping of an American reporter disappear from the news.

Funny, but Colin had always believed that all the news fit to print, and a lot that wasn't, was reported. Now he knew that there were things happening in the world that no one ever heard about.

Pulling the blue truck to a stop between his brother Dean's red pickup and his brother-in-law's green one, Colin contemplated the welcoming committee. Big enough, but there were still huge gaps in the Luchetti clan.

No Aaron — he was in Vegas. No Evan — Wisconsin this week. No Bobby — Lord only knew where he'd disappeared to.

Colin sighed and got out of the truck. His mother ran down the porch steps and threw herself into his arms.

She almost knocked him over. Eleanor Luchetti was a solid woman, and Colin had just spent several weeks eating bugs for dessert. He winced at the memories and buried his face in his mother's long, white braid.

She smelled like cookies. He must be home.

Never one for cuddling, she released him, but kept a hold of his hand as she led him to the house. There he was welcomed in turn by his dad, his sister, her husband, Dean and the two newest Luchettis.

His sister, Kim, held a little girl who was dressed to rival any of those in Marlie's preschool. An orange T-shirt with a black cat on the front covered black tights with tiny orange jack-o'-lanterns. She wore orange socks, an orange headband and black patent-leather mules. Why, he had no idea. The kid could barely walk.

"This is Glory," Kim said. "But call her Zsa Zsa. Everyone does."

Colin eyed the glitter on the child's cheekbones. "I can see why."

Brian, Kim's husband, snorted and earned a glare from his wife.

"I'm the Timinator."

A boy of about five danced along the edge of the top step. Dean reached out and yanked him back seconds before he would have tumbled down.

"You can call me Tim, though, and pretty soon you can call me Tim Luchetti, 'cause Dean's gonna make me his son."

Tim threw his arms around Dean's waist, then clambered up his leg in a monkey-like maneuver that had Colin's

327

eyes widening. He waited for Dean to say something sarcastic, but instead, his brother grinned and ruffled the boy's hair.

More had changed here than the seasons.

"Hungry, boy?" His dad held out his hand. When Colin took it, John pulled him into his arms for a rare hug. "You seem a little bony."

Colin shrugged. He didn't want to talk about what had happened. The ordeal could have been worse, but it had still been bad enough.

"I made cookies," his mom announced.

"All right!" Tim jumped from Dean's arms and banged through the front door.

The thud was followed by a hail of barking from the barn. Colin glanced that way and realized what had been missing from his homecoming.

"Bull and Bear?" he asked, referring to his father's dalmatians.

"Banished to the barn with the doodles." Kim shook her head. "You don't want to go there."

From the amount of sound, he had to agree.

Everyone filed into the house. Colin held back a minute, just staring at the fields and listening to the dogs, the cows, the pigs. Once he'd loathed the bucolic nature of this place. But while he'd been in a damp, dirty cell, the memory of it — and of Marlie — was all that had kept him sane.

Since being rescued by his brother, he'd picked up the phone a dozen times to call her. He'd always put it down again. His whole outlook had changed in Pakistan. When he thought he was going to die, he'd suddenly realized he hadn't been living. Not until he'd found her.

He wanted to tell Marlie that, but he wanted to tell her face-to-face.

Colin started as Dean spoke right behind him. "You okay?"

"I'll live."

His brother leaned against the porch railing and stared in the same direction Colin had been. "I've never seen you look at the farm like this before."

"I don't think I've ever seen it quite like this before."

"Whaddaya mean?"

"I always hated it. Couldn't wait to be gone."

"You and Kimmy both."

"Now she's back."

"And so are you."

"I'm not going to stay."

"Didn't think you would. But something's different. I don't think you'll be waltzing off to Portugal again anytime soon."

"Pakistan."

"Whatever."

"You're right. Although I do need to take a trip to Minneapolis, sooner rather than later."

"Marlie?"

"Yeah."

"In love with her?"

"Oh, yeah."

"Then what in hell are you doing here? Moron."

Colin smiled. There was the Dean he knew.

"Daddy?" Tim stood in the doorway, making puppy-dog eyes at Dean.

"Yeah?"

"Can I have another cookie?"

"How many have you had?"

"Five."

Dean snorted. "Dream on, buddy."

"I knew you'd say that." Tim stomped off in the direction of the barn.

"Daddy?" Colin shook his head. "I never thought I'd hear that word anywhere near you."

"Me neither, but it isn't half-bad. Kinda grows on you."

"Like moss?"

Dean shrugged. "Tim grew on me. Kid needed a dad. I needed . . . something. We fit."

Colin stared at his brother. Dean was different. Still sarcastic as hell and just a little bit cranky, but what he saw in Dean's eyes was something he'd never seen there before.

Happiness. Because of a kid he hadn't even known existed six months ago. Colin didn't get it.

"Can I ask you something?"

"Can I stop you?"

"You're going to change your life for a kid who's not yours?"

Dean's lips thinned. "He will be soon."

"Because a piece of paper says so?"

"Because I love him and he loves me."

"That's an awful big commitment."

"It's about time I made one."

"What if you meet a girl? What if she doesn't want two for the price of one?"

"Then she's not the right girl."

"Mmm."

"Listen, you got a problem with Tim?"

"Of course not."

"Then what's with all the questions?"

"I've had a lot of time to think . . . lately. And I just wondered what makes people want kids. I never did."

Dean watched Tim, who had released the doodles. Fluffy, spotted puppies and a giggling little boy rolled in the dirt, while Bull and Bear danced and barked on the sidelines.

"I never thought about kids," Dean murmured. "Never thought about marriage. I don't seem cut out for it."

Now that Dean mentioned it, Colin had rarely seen him with a girl. One in high school, another right after. There'd probably been more. Colin had always figured it would take a special woman to put up with Dean long enough to like him. He'd never considered that there might not be a woman special enough, and wasn't that sad?

Suddenly Colin ached for Marlie. He wished for perhaps the thousandth time that he'd headed straight north.

"Once Tim showed up," Dean continued, "it was like a part of my life that had been missing forever had finally arrived. Aaron says there are no accidents. Everything happens for a reason."

"Aaron would," Colin muttered.

Their almost-priest brother said stuff along those lines every day.

"Lately —" Dean stuck his hands in his

pockets and strolled off in the direction of the whirling doodles "— I think he's right."

Colin considered what his brother had said. No accidents. Everything happens for a reason. If so, what reason was there for what had happened to him in the past few months? He had no idea.

He should go inside, but it was so peaceful here. So fresh, so clean, so open and free. He continued to stare at the fields. It wasn't long before his mom joined him. She held a plateful of cookies.

"You're the most beautiful sight I've seen in months," he said.

She winced. "I don't want to think about what you've been looking at if that's the case."

"No, you don't, and if you don't mind, I'm not going to tell you. At least not yet."

"I suppose if I were a better mother, I'd want to know everything that happened. But I'm weak. I can't bear the thought of . . ." Her voice broke.

"Maybe I *should* tell you, then you won't wonder."

She smiled, cleared her throat and shoved the cookies at him again. "I'll pass."

He took the plate. "I'm alive. That's

more than a lot of kidnapped reporters can say."

"I know and we're grateful."

"So am I."

"It helps a lot to know Bobby's alive. Though not hearing from him makes me nervous, and having the army act like he's MIA makes me crazy."

"Me, too." He glanced at his mom. "I've been thinking a lot since Pakistan."

"I bet."

"About Bobby. About what he's up to."

"And?"

"I was thinking he might have been recruited for Delta Force."

She blinked. "The antiterrorist unit?"

"Yeah. They recruit out of Special Forces. They're into all sorts of shit no one knows about. The only other option is, he's gone rogue."

"Which means?"

"Flipped out. Off on his own. Rambo-style."

"He wouldn't."

Colin didn't think so, either, but there were a lot of things that had happened lately that he hadn't ever thought would occur.

"We don't have much choice now but to wait and see what happens."

"I hate waiting."

"Join the club." Colin bit into a cookie — chocolate chip and macadamia nut, his favorite. "Mom, if everyone ate your cookies, there'd be world peace."

"Sweet-talker." She patted his arm.

"I've got to go tomorrow."

"So soon?"

"Sorry. I'll come back."

"You're off to Minnesota?"

"Yeah."

"You want to tell me about her?"

"She's beautiful, sweet, giving." He swallowed. "She's everything I missed when I was in that place."

"Why didn't you snap her up before you left?"

"Because I'm an idiot."

"Mmm. That seems to be a common Luchetti ailment. Had a problem telling her you loved her, I suppose."

"No. Love wasn't the trouble."

"Really? That's new. What was?"

"I don't want kids."

"Excuse me?"

"Mom, I've always said that I didn't want kids. The world's screwed up enough."

"You're a psychic now? You somehow know that you'll be adding screwed-up kids to the mix?"

"Well, no. But life's rough — the world's a dangerous place."

"Always has been."

"Didn't you worry about bringing kids into that?"

"Of course. Worrying is what I do best."

"Me, too."

"Colin." She took his hand. "Kids are a chance to *improve* the world, not ruin it. You hope they do a better job than you did, hope they change things. Make what's wrong right. Or at least try." She squeezed his fingers. "My six little chances are doing okay so far. I'm proud of each and every one of you."

He thought about what she said. For quite a while.

"What else?" she pressed.

Trust his mom to see there was more.

"I'm no good with them. Kids don't like me, and I'm not all that keen on most of them, either."

"How can you not like a sweet baby or an adorable little boy like Tim?"

"I didn't say I didn't like them, exactly. I could take them or leave them. Preferably leave them, with someone else."

She snorted.

"What?"

"Sometimes you men are so dense. I

blame myself. Obviously I didn't explain life well enough."

"I thought that's what the polenta stick was for. Explaining."

"No, the polenta stick was for smacking you on the butt when you needed it."

"Too bad you broke it on Dean when he was eight."

"Too bad." She sighed. "I miss that stick. It was the perfect size. Now I have to resort to a spatula whenever someone needs an attitude adjustment."

"You used the spatula on Tim?"

She appeared insulted. "Never. He's my grandchild. I wouldn't lay a finger on him. I had to use the spatula on Aaron."

"Recently?"

"Of course."

Colin was sorry he hadn't been here for that.

"I figured once you met the right woman, you'd understand that *your* kids are different from just any old kid. Heck, I don't like anyone else's, either. There were plenty of times I didn't even like my own."

"Then why have them?"

She stared at him for a moment. "You really don't know?"

"Tell me."

"When you love someone with all your

heart, you want to make that love last for-ever. Kids are love come to life."

Love. Hope. A chance to change the world. Everything he'd dreamed of while in a cell.

"I've got to see Marlie," he said.

"I think you'd better."

CHAPTER NINETEEN

Marlie Anderson awoke on her wedding day with tears running down her cheeks. She had a feeling that was bad luck, but what wasn't?

She admitted it now. She'd been hoping against hope every day that Colin would turn up and sweep her away. Talk about chasing rainbows. What an impossible dream.

Marlie got out of bed, and though the world wavered a bit, at least she didn't feel the need to empty an already empty stomach. Maybe things were looking up.

She should be happy. She was going to have a husband and a family. Garth was her best friend, and he'd make a wonderful husband. Jake needed a mother. Her child needed a father. So why did she feel as if she was betraying everything she held dear?

"Marlie?" Her mother opened the door just a crack. "Can I come in?"

"Sure."

This was new. Her mom was awake before she was, and it wasn't even *Let's Make a Deal* Marathon Sunday.

Julie sat on the bed and handed Marlie a tissue-wrapped package. "These were your grandma's. And now they're yours."

Marlie unwrapped the paper. Inside lay a pearl necklace the same shade as the dress she'd chosen to be married in. Marlie recognized it from her parents' wedding pictures.

She fingered the pearls. They were beautiful and she'd often dreamed of wearing them on her wedding day. Holding them now, she felt like a thief and a fraud.

She handed them back to her mother. "I can't."

"What do you mean, you can't?"

Marlie hadn't told her mom the true reason she was marrying Garth. Her mom had assumed the baby was his, and Marlie had let her. She hadn't been up to the task of explaining every mistake she'd made. Today she felt better, stronger, so she did.

Her mom stared at her. "Have you lost your mind?"

"Excuse me?"

"Please tell me you didn't say what I thought you said."

"What did I say?"

"That you're marrying a man you don't love for the sake of the children."

"Is that a crime?"

"It is when you're in love with someone else."

"Colin and I want two different things. Our marriage would be a disaster. I can't do that to our child, can't do it to him or to me. Sometimes a person has to be practical."

"Don't you think Colin has a right to know about the baby?" Julie asked.

"Of course. I never said I'd keep the child from him. I just plan to tell him after the wedding."

"When it's too late for him to do anything."

"I don't want him to *have* to do anything. I don't want anything from him."

"Maybe that's your problem. You expect too little, so that's exactly what you get."

Marlie stood and paced the room. "He told me how he felt about children. He doesn't want any. Ever." She shoved her fingers through her tangled hair. "I love this child already. Colin will only see it as a mistake, an accident, a burden. A blight on society. I can't do that to my baby. Garth is a good father. The best. I want that for my child."

"The best thing for your child is a father and a mother who are happy."

"I'm happy!"

341

She would have been more convincing if her voice hadn't cracked.

Her mother shook her head. "Marlie. Sweetie. You break my heart."

"I've thought this through. He can't live here — I can't follow him everywhere. He shouldn't have to give up what he's worked for his entire life."

"Why does it have to be one or the other? Isn't there some kind of compromise?"

"So I stay here and I wait and I wait and I wait? Then someday Chief Moose knocks on my door to tell me he's dead? I'll pass, thanks."

Silence settled over the room. Marlie wanted to take back her words, but it was too late.

"You've let my nightmare become yours. I'm sorry."

"No, Mom. I'm sorry."

"I know you think I'm crazy."

"Mom —"

"Maybe I am. I'd rather watch TV than stare out the window waiting for your dad's truck to come up the road. I know he's gone. But some days it's easier to pretend that I'm still waiting."

"I can't do that. My child is going to have a father who won't leave, a father who loves him and wants him and thinks that he's the best idea since electricity. I can give my child that in Garth."

"So you're going through with this."

Marlie stared her mom in the eye, lifted her chin and said, "Yes."

Wind Lake appeared asleep. The streets were empty. A lot of the stores were closed. Had someone died?

He went straight to Marlie's, knocked on the door. No one answered. That was strange. Julie never went anywhere. She might miss *Name That Tune*.

He peeked in the windows. No one was there.

Colin looked up, then down Briar Lane. If he didn't know better, he'd think he was in the middle of a horror movie. One where all the inhabitants of a sleepy Midwestern town disappeared.

Beginning to feel creeped out, he hurried downtown and went straight to the *Weekly*. Mick would know what was up.

The press was pumping; the noise was deafening. Colin just stood there and enjoyed it.

Mick came out from the back, saw him and grinned. He said something, which Colin couldn't hear over the din, so he cupped his ear and mouthed, "What?"

The old man crossed the room, slapped him on the back and drew him outside. "You got here just in time."

"For?"

Mick's face creased into a ferocious scowl. "You don't know?"

"About?"

"The wedding."

Da-dum!

Soap-opera music punctuated the sucker punch to Colin's gut.

"What wedding?"

Mick reached into his shirt pocket and pulled out a piece of newsprint. Colin saw Marlie's somewhat tense smile seconds before he read, "Anderson-Lundquist Nuptials."

"Hell. What is she thinking?"

"I wondered that myself. She's been walking around like a ghost. Seemed sick half the time. Not like herself at all. She's always been such a cheery young thing."

Guilt swamped Colin. Marlie had been sad and sick because of him. Maybe he should just leave, let her marry Garth and have the safe, boring life she'd always dreamed of.

"Oh, no, you don't." Mick grabbed his arm.

"Don't what?"

"You were thinking about leaving."

"So?"

"I'm gonna tell you a little story."

"Do you have to?"

"Yes. Now shut up and listen." Mick cracked his knuckles. "Once upon a time there was a guy who wanted to be a newspaperman. He devoted so much energy to that dream that he didn't have time for anything or anyone else. That was fine with him, until one day he looked up and realized he was old and alone. He had no one to leave his business to, no one to retire with. He was going to die someday soon, and no one would care."

"The moral of the story is?"

"What the hell do you think it is? There's more to life than work. More to bein' happy than bein' successful. If I'd had a chance like you have now, I'd have grabbed it with both hands."

"What chance is that?"

"Get your butt to the church and stop that wedding or you'll be sorry for the rest of your life."

Mick was right. He had to try.

"Which way?" he asked.

"End of the block and turn right."

Colin ran faster than he'd ever run in his

life. Even so, he was just getting to the steps of the church when the bells began to ring. The doors slammed open and people streamed out.

He was too late.

Marlie sat in the little room off the vestibule and waited.

The door opened and shut. She couldn't bring herself to meet his eyes.

"I'm sorry," she whispered. "I thought I could, but I can't."

"I know." Garth laid his big hands on her shoulders. "I shouldn't have pushed you. I just wanted to have a family again so badly, but it wouldn't be the same, would it?"

"No. What you and Nika had was special. You deserve love, Garth, and I can't love you that way."

"Because you love him."

"Yeah." She reached up and tangled their fingers together. "Still best friends?"

"Always and forever." He kissed the top of her head. "Jake wants to talk to you."

Her heart lurched. "Low blow, Lundquist."

"Isn't it?" Garth gave her one final squeeze and left the room.

Marlie wasn't sure what she was going to

do now. Maybe she'd sell her house and her business, pack up her mom and get out of Dodge. Once, everything she'd needed was right here. Without Colin, Wind Lake was no longer enough.

The door opened and shut. Little-boy feet thunked across the room. Jake plopped into her lap. Dressed in a miniature tuxedo, he had his hair slicked back. He smelled like little-boy sweat — a scent reminiscent of sunshine.

"You don't want to be my mom?" His lip trembled.

Marlie cast her eyes heavenward and prayed for inspiration. One of the reasons she'd called off the wedding was for Jake. He was a product of the complete love and devotion of two people. He deserved better than she could give him.

When she'd heard the wedding march, Marlie had realized she wouldn't be able to spend a lifetime pretending she was Garth's wife when she was only his friend. And the one who would be hurt the most was Jake.

But how could she explain future pain to a little boy who was hurting so badly right now?

"Of course I want to be your mom, Big Jake. But there's complications."

Jake frowned. "What's so complicated about me lovin' you and you lovin' me?"

If it could only be that simple.

"It's not the love that's complicated."

"Then be my mommy. Ned's, too. We need one. Bad." He batted his eyelashes and made the saddest face she'd ever seen.

"You've got a mommy, sweetheart. Just because she went to heaven too soon doesn't make her any less your mom."

"I know. But I want a mommy who isn't in heaven. I want you."

"And you've got me. I will always be your friend. Always."

He sighed. "It's not the same."

True. But right now it was the best she could do.

"I promise I won't wet the mat or the bed. I'll make Ned go away, too."

"Jake." Marlie took his sweet face in both hands and held him nose to nose. "You have nothing to do with what happened today. You'll stop wetting the bed when you're ready, and Ned will go away when you don't need him anymore." She snuck a quick kiss to his nose and let him go. "Trust me."

He made a face and rubbed her kiss off with the back of his hand.

"You'd better run back to your dad. He

needs a hug, and I've got a houseful of wedding gifts to return."

"You gotta give back the presents?" He jumped down from her lap. "That sucks."

She opened her mouth to rebuke him for his language — somehow *sucks* from a five-year-old seemed like a curse — but the door opened again.

"I knew it was your fault," Jake muttered.

There was a thud, then an exclamation of pain before the door slammed once more.

Marlie spun around. Colin was hopping on one foot and clinging to his shin.

"He kicked me."

Colin had been an expert at hand-to-hand combat since he was two, but today he hadn't even seen the blow coming.

Marlie stared at him, wide-eyed. She didn't cry out, run to him, declare everlasting devotion. Why would she? She was all dressed up to marry another man.

He stopped hopping, let his foot fall back to the floor. His gaze wandered over her from head to toe.

"You're so pretty," he whispered.

"You're so blind." She turned away.

Colin stood in the doorway, uncertain

what to do or say to make this right.

The wedding was off. He'd garnered that much as he'd pushed his way desperately into the church, even before he'd run straight into Garth.

The big man had grabbed him by the shirt and slammed him against the wall. "Hurt her and die," he'd growled.

"Urgh," had been Colin's answer.

Garth let him go, then walked out of the church without a backward glance.

"What are you doing here, Colin?"

She stood facing him, her back straight as if she was prepared for a battle.

There was something about her, something different. She was pale, and her face was a little bit thinner. Her eyes, behind a set of new, smaller glasses, were sad. But that wasn't what made him continue to stare at her and ignore her pointed question. Suddenly, as if he'd been hit by a bolt of lightning, he knew.

"You're having my baby," he blurted.

"Garth is gonna die." She headed for the door.

"Whoa, Xena." He put his arm out, and she stopped centimeters from running into it. "Garth didn't tell me."

"Who did?"

"No one."

"Then how . . . ?"

He shrugged. "I just looked at you and I knew."

She rolled her eyes and turned away.

"It's true?" He held his breath, hoping against hope that her answer would be yes, which surprised him almost more than the revelation did. His mother was right. He *wanted* their baby. The very thought filled him with such joy he could barely keep from touching her.

Marlie's shoulders slumped. "It's true."

The light dawned. "That's why you were marrying Garth."

"Partly." She glanced at him. "But don't worry. I don't want anything from you. I don't expect anything."

Every word was like another kick to his sore shin. "I guess I deserve that."

"What are you doing here?" she repeated.

In that moment he understood what Aaron had meant when he said everything happened for a reason. If Colin hadn't been taken prisoner by Pakistani terrorists, he never would have seen that his job was just a job while Marlie was his world.

"I adore you. I can't live without you. I don't want to be away from you ever again."

Pain flashed in her eyes. "Colin, don't. We've been over this and love isn't enough."

He had to touch her; he couldn't wait any longer. He stepped forward, meaning to fold her into his arms, but instead, his hands went to her waist, a palm slid across her belly. She froze and lifted her gaze to his.

"Don't send me away. Please. I want everything you dreamed of."

"Since when?"

"Since I thought my life was over."

Tears sparked her eyes. "Oh, Colin."

Her hand covered his.

"When I was in that place, all I thought was that I'd lived my life, and what did I have to show for it? A few awards, some articles. Big deal."

"It is a big deal."

"No." He flexed his fingers, stroked her skin through the satin dress. "*This* is a big deal. The biggest deal of my life. Our life. I love you. I need you. You're the only thing that kept me breathing over there. I should have come to you right away, but I was afraid."

"Of me?"

"I was afraid you'd say no and then what would I do?"

"I don't know, what?"

"Go back to my pathetic life — no ties, no responsibilities, no home. If I had to do that, I may as well have stayed in that cell."

She winced. "You were in a cell?"

"I've been in a cell all my life. You were the key."

"Corny."

"But true. Marry me?"

She hesitated and his heart flopped down to his feet. "Do you still want me to travel with you?"

"Hell, no!"

His voice was too loud and too vehement. But the thought of what might have happened if she'd gone with him when he'd asked the last time turned his blood to ice. He'd seen so many horrible things, and they hadn't bothered him — much — until he thought of them coming near her.

"My traveling days are done. This last trip kind of took all the fun out of it. Forever."

"I'm sorry."

"I'm not."

"What are you going to do here?"

"Make babies?"

She laughed, and the sound was the one he remembered. Pure joy, sunshine in shadow, the sound that he'd heard in the depths of his despair.

"While you're very good at it," she said, "I don't think there's much cash in the practice."

"Don't worry, I'll think of something."

"I'm sure you will."

"Is that a yes?"

"I'm still considering the offer."

He grasped for something else to say, anything to get her to agree. "You know, I never collected on that debt you owe me."

"What debt?"

"I won Ghost in the Graveyard."

"Oh, that." She shrugged as if it meant nothing.

"You're a welsher?"

"Of course not! What do you want?"

"You. Forever."

"Well, if that's what you *really* want . . ."

He pulled her closer and placed his hand over their child. "It's what I really want."

She stared into his eyes, considered his face, thought about it for a while, then smiled.

"Me, too."

EPILOGUE

"I'm nervous." Marlie fidgeted in the passenger seat of Colin's black pickup truck.

"They'll love you. Relax."

"Why don't *you* try meeting your in-laws when you're four months pregnant?"

"If I could, honey, I would."

She punched him.

They were going to the Luchetti farm for Christmas. His family didn't know about the baby yet. The news was something Colin had decided he'd rather tell them in person. Marlie had to agree.

But they were married. Colin hadn't wasted any time. As soon as he'd gotten the license, he'd hauled her in front of a priest.

She'd worn her grandmother's pearls, then tucked them away in her jewelry case for their daughter.

Marlie let her hand fall to her barely swollen belly. She didn't know if this was a daughter or a son, and she didn't care. She'd have both eventually.

Life was going well. Colin had called to quit his job at the *Dispatch*, and got an earful from his boss.

"Since when do you write humor pieces?" she'd demanded.

Seemed that Gerry had gotten hold of one of Colin's articles for the *Weekly*. She'd loved it. So had her pals. She'd called in the favor he owed her. Colin's new column — an on-the-road-type piece in the tradition of his hero Ernie Pyle — was going to be in syndication throughout the country by spring.

They'd made the upper floor of the Anderson house into an office and a nursery. He was going to watch her mother and the baby while Marlie watched the children of Wind Lake grow.

He'd also promised to help Mick at the *Weekly* on the days the paper went to press. For reasons she couldn't fathom, Colin loved that old printing press almost as much as he loved her.

Colin turned the truck onto a long, rutted, winding lane that led to a picturesque farm. Three silver silos rose out of the flat land, an American flag waving on top of each one. Nearby stood a three-story stone farmhouse and various white-plank outbuildings.

As the truck slowed in front of the house, the porch filled with people and their pickup was surrounded by dogs.

Colin rolled down the window. "Would someone call the doodles off?"

A little boy separated from the others and ran toward the barn whistling. The dogs raced after him.

Colin shut off the engine. Marlie took a deep breath. Together they got out of the car.

They were welcomed into the Luchetti house, the Luchetti family, with hugs and kisses and laughter.

Dean, Kim, Brian, Zsa Zsa, John, Tim — so many names, so many faces. At least she had a lifetime to sort them out.

Colin's dad tried to tell her a knock-knock joke, but before he could get past the second "knock," everyone groaned.

"What?" he asked. "I gotta know if she's one of us."

"One of you," Colin muttered. "No one likes your jokes except Kim."

"Zsa Zsa likes them," Kim pointed out.

"Zsa Zsa talks to her shoes," Dean said.

Marlie smiled. This was just the kind of family she'd always dreamed of. Large, loud, affectionate — even the teasing was nice. She wanted to belong so badly she could taste it.

"Marlie's one of us." Colin put his arm

around her. "It says so on her driver's license."

But a change in her name didn't make her one of them. Not yet.

"Where's Mom?" Colin asked.

"She'll be right out," John said. "She's just finishing the potatoes in the kitchen."

"Come on." Colin took Marlie's hand and led her to the back of the house.

He pushed open the swinging door. A sturdy woman with a long, white braid stirred pots and hummed.

"Mom?" Colin said. "Meet Marlie."

His mother turned. Her welcoming smile froze and her eyes went straight to Marlie's middle. She picked up a spatula and smacked Colin on the forehead.

"Can just one of my children get married and *then* get someone pregnant? Hmm?"

Colin rubbed his face. "Too late."

"I can see that."

"It was my fault," Marlie blurted.

Eleanor Luchetti's blue eyes, so much like Colin's, flicked toward her. She tapped her foot against the floor in the same rhythm she tapped the spatula against her palm. "You don't say."

Marlie stepped in front of Colin and lifted her chin. "I do say."

Eleanor's mouth twitched. Her eyes softened. She laid down the spatula. "Welcome to the family."

And just like that, Marlie's name became Luchetti.

Later that night as they lay in the bunk beds that had once been Colin's and Bobby's, Marlie contemplated her life, and it was good.

The only darkness on their horizon was the continued absence of Bobby. It was the darkness on every Luchetti's horizon.

"I think Jake's warming up to me." Colin sat down on her bed and reached into his duffel bag.

"Oh?"

"He was over this afternoon talking, questioning, being a kid."

"Uh-huh."

Marlie sat back and waited.

"Ack!"

Colin jumped up, hit his head on the underside of the bed, dropped his bag, and Houdini came shooting out. As her big, bad husband climbed on to the top bunk, she watched the guinea pig race around the room.

Colin's sheepish face appeared over the edge of the mattress. "I tried to get over my irrational fear in prison, but I guess it didn't work."

"There were guinea pigs in prison?"

"Rats."

She shuddered. Colin hadn't talked much about his time in Pakistan. Every once in a while, like now, a tidbit slipped out, and that was fine with her. Marlie wasn't sure she'd be able to handle the entire story all at once.

Houdini stopped running and stared up at Colin, nose twitching.

"I think he likes you," Marlie ventured.

"I don't like him. Will Jake ever stop hiding that rodent in my things?"

"I doubt it."

Colin fell back on the bed with a groan and Marlie grinned.

She'd been chasing rainbows all of her life, but she'd never found one until she'd found him.